D1115305

Other books by Carol Ellis
you will enjoy:

The Stepdaughter

The Window

My Secret Admirer

CAROL ELLIS

SCHOLASTIC INC.
New York Toronto London Auckland Sydney

No part of this publication may be reproduced in whole or in part, or stored in a retrieval system, or transmitted in any form or by any means, electronic, mechanical, photocopying, recording, or otherwise, without written permission of the publisher. For information regarding permission, write to Scholastic Inc., 730 Broadway, New York, NY 10003.

ISBN 0-590-46411-6

12 11 10 9 8 7 6 5 4 3   4 5 6 7 8/9

Printed in the U.S.A.   01

First Scholastic printing, July 1993

Prologue

The sky was just beginning to get light when the six campers crawled out of their tents. They were about the same age, ten and eleven years old. A counselor joined them, and they stood together in a little clump for a minute, yawning and shivering in the cool air. Then they started walking away from the campsite, while the rest of the campers still slept in their tents. They were looking for dry twigs and branches for a camp fire. That was their job this morning, the last morning of Camp Silverlake's three-day wilderness hike. It had been fun, but they were getting a little tired of roughing it. Later they'd go back to the campground and hang out in their cabins. They'd eat junk food and go swimming in the lake. But first, they had to get wood for a fire so everyone could have breakfast.

It had rained during the night, and finding

dry wood wasn't easy. Their search took them deeper into the pine forest, so tall and thick the rain would have had trouble getting through the towering canopy of branches. The sun was up now, and the birds had been awake for hours. But it was still shadowy under the trees.

The carpet of pine needles was soft and slick. One of the campers decided to see if he could slide on them. He took a running start and actually slid a few feet. But then his front foot caught on something — a stump, maybe, or some twisted undergrowth. Before he could stop, he went tumbling out of sight.

The counselor and the other campers called to him to make sure he was all right. There was no answer. They shouted again, and still he didn't answer. They hurried along, and found him at the edge of a deep gully. His hair and the back of his shirt were covered with pine needles, but he didn't look hurt. He was just sitting there. He had his knees drawn up and his arms wrapped around them. He didn't answer when the others talked to him. He kept staring down into the gully. So finally, everyone else did, too.

The trees weren't as thick here, and long shafts of sunlight reached down into the gully. At the bottom was a fallen tree. Its trunk was huge, partly buried in decaying leaves. A squirrel scampered along its length, stopped, and eyed the campers nervously. They didn't notice.

They'd finally seen what the other camper was staring at.

Slammed up against the trunk of the tree was a body, wearing jeans and a T-shirt. One of the feet was bare. The shirt was royal blue, with silver letters on the back spelling CAMP SILVERLAKE.

Everyone was still. So still, the squirrel must have decided they were harmless. It scrabbled along the trunk another foot. Then it hopped onto the back of the body and looked up at the campers again.

Someone screamed. It was thin and high-pitched at first, but then it got stronger and louder. The squirrel ran off and the birds grew silent. When the piercing scream died down, the only sound was the sighing of the wind high above in the tops of the pine trees.

Chapter 1

Seven Years Later

I was so sure. Even after so much time, I was sure everyone would feel something. I haven't forgotten what happened and I know they remember, too. I thought it would show in their faces, but it doesn't. They smile and laugh. Their faces are happy.

It's peaceful here. Quiet and calm. They're happy. They don't feel anything, and they think there's nothing to be afraid of.

It won't last.

The camp fire was starting to die down, but nobody seemed ready to call it a night. Rachel Owens stifled a yawn and glanced around at the other counselors. None of them looked sleepy, but maybe they were all used to mountain air. She yawned again, squeezing her eyes shut. When she opened them, she saw a charred marshmallow about six inches from her nose. It was on the end of a stick. The hand holding the stick belonged to a guy named Jordan Hurley.

"Pure sugar," Jordan said with a friendly smile. "It'll help keep you awake."

Rachel took the stick and slid the marshmallow into her mouth. "I think I need the whole bag," she said after she'd swallowed. "I'm still sleepy."

"Not good." Jordan sounded serious, but his blue eyes were teasing. "If you don't have any energy, you'll never be able to handle all the little campers when they get here. They'll run circles around you."

Across the camp fire, Steve Michaels laughed. Steve was tall, with a long face and thick, sandy hair. He always seemed to be laughing at something — or *someone*. "Jordan's right, Rachel," he said. "You lose control of them, you're in for a lot of grief."

"You make them sound like a bunch of terrorists," Rachel said.

"Steve knows," Mark James said. His white-blond hair was like a halo in the firelight. "Steve was one himself."

Paul Sidney leaned back on his elbows. "Steve was a terrorist?"

Linda Dolan nudged Rachel in the arm. "Don't listen to them," she said. She brushed back a strand of long red hair and smiled with wide amber-colored eyes. "For most of the kids, it'll be their first time at a sleep-away camp. You know how that feels."

Teresa Montrose nodded. "They'll be too scared and homesick to make any trouble." Terry was small, with short dark hair and a shy smile. "The first time I went to camp, I cried myself to sleep for three nights." Rachel noted that Terry still seemed a bit scared and homesick.

"Well, I hope they're not all a bunch of cry-babies," Stacey Brunswick said, tossing her blonde hair off her shoulder. "That could get boring."

Tim and Michelle laughed. They were in their twenties, the head counselors in charge of the others. "Bored's the last thing you'll get, Stacey," Tim said. "You'll be too busy."

"Speaking of busy," Michelle said, "let's talk about tomorrow's schedule."

It would be a week before the campers arrived, and the ten counselors would spend that time getting Camp Silverlake in shape for them. Getting it in shape included painting and cleaning, checking trails, testing and repairing the boats, and planning activities like the three-day wilderness hike that came near the end of the camping session.

Several more older counselors would arrive

sometime before camp opened. Meanwhile, Tim and Michelle were in charge of Rachel and the other seven teenage counselors.

It felt sort of like being a camper again herself, Rachel thought — thrown together with seven kids she didn't know, wondering how they'd like her and how she'd like them. She looked around at the people she'd be spending the week with. Terry didn't say much, she was shy and withdrawn — not the type of person Rachel would have expected as a camp counselor. Linda was the opposite — outgoing and friendly and into organizing things. It had been her idea to have a cookout tonight, and the first thing she'd done when she arrived was rearrange the cots in the girls' cabin so there'd be more room to move around. As long as she didn't get too bossy, Rachel didn't mind.

She wasn't sure how she felt about Stacey. Stacey complained a lot: The cot was uncomfortable, even with her air mattress on it; the latrines were smelly; there was poison ivy all over the place. But Rachel had to admit she was generous. She'd stocked their cabin with enough food to last them through a siege — cookies and potato chips and trail mix — and told the others to help themselves.

Rachel hadn't made up her mind about the

guys either. Mark seemed kind of cold, and a little arrogant. Steve was like every goof-off she'd ever met. The little kids would probably love him. Jordan was good-looking, and a really nice guy so far. Paul? Dark brown hair, hazel eyes. Very serious, always watching. He made her a little uncomfortable.

But it was too soon to tell about any of them, really. She was always doing that — making judgments about people before she got to know them and then being surprised when they turned out to be different. For all she knew, Stacey could become her best friend there.

As for Camp Silverlake, Rachel loved it already. When she'd first seen it earlier in the day, she decided it was going to be a great place to spend five weeks of the summer before college. The pay wasn't great, but the scenery was gorgeous. A mountain lake, incredibly tall trees, miles of trails, and air spiced with the scent of pine. Cold air, now that the sun was gone and the fire was dying. Rachel shivered and pulled the sleeves of her sweatshirt over her hands.

"I'm cold, too," Stacey said when she noticed Rachel shiver. "I still don't know what we're doing out here. There's a perfectly warm lodge we could be sitting in."

Linda laughed. "Okay, Stacey, I won't suggest anymore cookouts. I just thought it would be fun."

"Yeah, Stace. We'll be eating in the lodge most of the time, anyway." Steve poked a stick in the embers and watched the sparks fly up. "Besides, you shouldn't complain. You'll set a bad example for the kiddies."

"The kiddies aren't here yet," Stacey said, wrapping her arms around her knees. "I thought I'd have some privileges once I got to be a counselor."

"You do," Steve told her. "You get to use the private showers in the lodge. Campers have to use the showers out by the cabins, remember?"

Rachel had figured out earlier from listening to everyone talk that Stacey, Mark, Steve, Jordan, and Paul had gone to Camp Silverlake when they were kids. They all remembered each other, but they didn't act like good friends. At first Rachel thought it was because they lived in different towns, and the camp was really their only connection.

But it wasn't just that. There was a strange kind of tension among them, even when they were joking around.

"How could I forget the showers?" Stacey said with a shudder. "Cement floor and spiders

10

in the corners." She shuddered again. "I hated those spiders."

"Personally, I didn't like the racoons and stuff prowling around at night," Mark said.

"What do you mean by 'stuff'?" Terry asked nervously. "Not bears, I hope."

"Worse," Steve said. He lowered his voice and made a ghoulish face. "Does anybody remember Mr. Drummond?"

"Oh, don't remind me!" Stacey said. "He was so creepy!"

"You'd better keep your voices down," Tim warned. "He's somewhere around."

"You mean he still works here?"

Tim nodded.

Mark and Steve groaned. Stacey peered out at the surrounding darkness, her shoulders hunched.

"Isn't somebody going to tell the rest of us who Mr. Drummond is?" Rachel asked. "I'm starting to get nervous."

"Don't be," Paul told her. "Mr. Drummond's kind of the caretaker, I guess you'd call him."

"He helps keep up the grounds, checks the place in the winter, fixes pipes, drives down for supplies if there's an emergency, stuff like that," Tim explained.

"And he's harmless," Paul added, looking at Rachel. "He just keeps to himself."

"It's the way he looks," Stacey said. "He's big and tall and bald. And he has little beady eyes and he never smiles."

"Yeah, well, Paul's right, though," Tim said. "He's harmless and he works hard. He's been with the camp for about fifteen years and nobody's ever complained."

"Nobody but every camper who ever went here," Stacey said. "I remember we used to scare ourselves to death at night. Every time there'd be a sound outside our cabin, one of us would decide it was Drummond and we'd all dive into our sleeping bags and hide."

"You mean you didn't make somebody go out and look?" Jordan asked.

"Right, that's what *we* did," Steve said. "We drew straws to see who had to go out in the dark. I had to do it once, but after that, we made sure — " Steve suddenly broke off. He'd been smiling, but now the smile was gone. Rachel saw him look around, his eyes darting nervously back and forth.

"You made sure what?" Paul asked.

Stacey cleared her throat loudly. Steve glanced at Jordan. Jordan shrugged and looked the other way.

It was Mark who answered. "We made sure there were always fresh batteries in the flashlight."

Mark and Steve laughed, but Rachel didn't think they were really amused. It was like some unspoken message had been passed.

A message to keep their secret to themselves.

Chapter 2

Rachel looked at everyone else. Linda was laughing with the others, and Terry was smiling uncertainly. Paul was turning a stick around and around in his fingers, frowning at the fire. When he glanced up and caught Rachel watching him, he stared back at her, his hazel eyes thoughtful. He wasn't really looking at her, though. He seemed to be working something out in his mind.

Mark stood up then and stretched lazily. "I don't know about the rest of you guys, but I've had it for the night."

Everyone else agreed, and after making sure the fire was out, they headed for bed. Tim and Michelle would be in the lodge, but everyone else was staying in the same cabins the campers would stay in when they got here, the girls in one, the guys in another.

Walking away from the rocky beach near the

lake, Rachel found herself in step with Jordan. "You don't look sleepy anymore," he said, peering at her face in the darkness.

"I'm not," she laughed. "There's nothing like sitting around a camp fire hearing about bears and strange noises and scary groundskeepers to wake you right up."

"I don't think you have to worry about bears," Jordan said. "I guess they're around, but nobody ever saw one." He leaned his head close to hers. "Scary noises, though, that's something else," he whispered. "You'll hear plenty of those."

"Thanks a lot." Rachel punched him lightly on the arm. "At least you won't catch me walking around in the dark, not even with a flashlight."

"Yeah, well. We were just kids then, what can I say?" Jordan's eyes narrowed and he didn't sound amused anymore. "Didn't you ever do anything dumb when you were a kid?"

"Lots of things." Suddenly he seemed so serious. Rachel couldn't figure out what the problem was. "In fact, believe it or not, I still do dumb things. Not very often, of course," she added jokingly.

Jordan's mood shifted again and he laughed. "Of course," he said. He nudged her with his shoulder, then headed off toward the guys' cabin. "See you tomorrow, Rachel."

Rachel stopped and watched him as he walked away from her. She liked his hair, dark-blond and thick. He seemed kind of moody, though, going from cheerful to serious and back to cheerful so fast she had trouble keeping up. She'd never liked moody people or, at least, people who wouldn't bother to explain their moods. But maybe Jordan wasn't really like that. After all, she'd just met him a few hours ago.

By now, Jordan had gone into his cabin, and Rachel suddenly realized everyone else was gone, too. She was standing alone. She looked up past the tops of the pines, her head tilted as far back as it would go. There was no moon tonight. There were plenty of stars, but they didn't look soft and twinkly. They looked cold, glittering like chips of ice.

Shivering, Rachel looked down and took a step toward her cabin.

That's when she heard the sound.

It was coming from one of the paths that led from the cabins to the lodge. But all the paths were bordered by trees and she couldn't see well in the inky darkness.

She could hear just fine, though. And what she heard were footsteps.

Tim or Michelle, coming to see if everyone

was okay? Maybe. But the footsteps were heavy and shuffling, snapping twigs and scattering pebbles. Michelle was tiny, like Terry, and Tim was tall but kind of skinny. Neither one of them would walk like that.

Rachel started walking fast, snapping twigs under her own feet. When she was almost to the cabin, she tripped on a root and went sprawling on her hands and knees. As she scrambled up, she turned and chanced a look behind her.

The path she'd been on was still dark. But not so dark that she couldn't see the figure moving along it.

Not a bear, after all. A person.

Chapter 3

With a gasp, Rachel spun around and practically leaped the last few feet to the cabin door. She shouldered it open with a bang, then slammed it shut and leaned against it. The hanging bulb with its green, cone-shaped shade swung back and forth, making wild swooping shadows along the wood-slatted walls.

The other three girls stopped what they'd been doing and stared. Stacey, sitting cross-legged on one of the narrow beds with a jumble of clothes spread around her and a hairbrush in her hair, finally asked, "What happened to you?"

Rachel gasped for breath and tried to laugh. She knew she must look kind of wild. "This is crazy, but I was walking back and I heard somebody on one of the paths. I got so scared, I almost screamed."

"Well, who was it?" Linda asked. "One of

the guys playing a trick, I bet."

Rachel shook her head. "I'm pretty sure it was Mr. Drummond. I couldn't see if he was bald, but he was tall. And big, like Stacey said."

"No kidding?" Stacey pulled the brush the rest of the way through her hair and got off the bed. Reaching for the chain, she turned the light off, plunging the cabin into total darkness.

"What are you doing?" Terry asked anxiously.

"I just want to see." Moving across the narrow width of the cabin, Stacey pulled back the green cloth shade on one of the screened windows. "Wow. I forgot how dark it gets out here."

"Let's turn the light back on," Terry said. "This is making me nervous."

"Just a sec, I think I see him," Stacey whispered.

The quiet stillness of the night was suddenly broken by the sound Rachel had heard — the heavy-footed steps of someone walking on the path.

"Can you see anything?" Linda whispered.

"Yeah," Stacey breathed softly. "It's Drummond, all right. He's coming this way!"

The footsteps grew louder and heavier. Then they stopped. Suddenly, a beam of light flashed onto the window shade. Rachel heard Stacey gasp and duck down. The light disappeared and footsteps crunched toward the cabin door. Rachel was still leaning against it, but she hadn't latched it. She turned and fumbled for the hook in the dark. She was trying to fit it into place when the footsteps stopped and a voice called out, "Everything all right in there?"

The voice was deep and strong, the kind of voice that went with the man Rachel had seen a few moments ago. She slid the hook into place, making it rattle.

"Hey, everything okay?" the voice called.

"Somebody answer him before he barges in here," Stacey hissed.

Someone cleared her throat. Then Linda's voice called back, "Everything's fine, Mr. Drummond. Just fine, thanks."

"Good. Just checking. Didn't mean to disturb you." Gravel crunched again, and then the heavy footsteps faded away.

Everyone waited in silence for a moment, hardly breathing. Then Rachel heard Stacey move again, and suddenly the hanging light was pulled on.

"I told you he was creepy," Stacey said. Her cheek was crisscrossed with the pattern of the window screen. "I think we should bar the door."

"But what was he doing out there?" Terry asked, her voice tense.

"Checking the camp out, making sure everything's all right." Stacey said. "It's part of his job, or so they always told us. I still think we should bar the door."

"There's nothing to bar it with," Linda said. She moved to her bed and sat down, pushing her long red hair back with her hands. "Besides, Tim said Mr. Drummond's okay. They wouldn't have let him work here for fifteen years if he wasn't. He said he was checking things out and that's all he did. There's no sense scaring ourselves."

"I guess maybe Linda's right," Terry said. She hefted a big duffel bag onto her bed and started unpacking it.

"What about you, Rachel?" Stacey asked. "You saw the guy. Do you really think he's okay?"

"I suppose so," Rachel said. She stretched out on her bed and stared up at the ceiling. "I mean he scared me, but maybe if I'd just stuck around and said hello, he would have turned out to be real nice."

"Yeah, sure. A real nice, bald-headed giant." Stacey shrugged her shoulders and flopped onto her bed. "Well, okay. But if anything happens, don't say I didn't warn you."

"Did anything ever happen when you were here before?" Linda asked.

Stacey lifted her head. "What do you mean?" she asked sharply.

"I mean with Mr. Drummond." Linda smiled. "That's who we're talking about, isn't it?"

"Oh. Yeah." Stacey let her head fall back. "No, nothing happened, but that doesn't mean it won't. But let's just forget it, okay?" She sat up and started brushing her hair again. "Actually, Rachel, when you didn't come back to the cabin with us, I thought you and Jordan had snuck off somewhere. Private, you know. I saw you walking with him."

Rachel shook her head.

"You're not interested in him?" Stacey asked.

Rachel laughed, a little embarrassed. "I don't know. Maybe."

"I kind of like Steve," Linda said. "Not that I'm interested," she added. "I'm already going with somebody." She unzipped one of her bags and pulled out a small snapshot of her boyfriend which she showed around.

It turned out that Teresa had a boyfriend, too. Instead of a snapshot, she'd brought a five-by-eight photograph in a silver frame, which she put on the shelf above her bed.

"Well, it looks like you and I have our pick, Rachel," Stacey said. "Steve and Mark are fun. Jordan's kind of wishy-washy, but he's really cute."

"Mark's fun?" Rachel asked. "He acts like he's above it all."

"He's so tall, he is," Terry said with a little laugh. "Of course, almost everybody's tall next to me."

"Mark's really smart," Stacey said. "I mean, like a genius or something. Paul's good-looking, but he's *so* serious. He was always like that."

"Oh, that's right," Linda said. "You know him from before. You were all happy campers together."

Stacey stared at Linda for a moment, as if she thought Linda was being sarcastic. Then she shrugged. "I didn't know him very well," she said. "I mean, I didn't get to know any of them very well. They might as well be strangers."

"And maybe they've changed. I know I'm not the same person I was when I was eleven," Linda said. She stood up, yawning and stretching. "Is anybody else sleepy?"

"I've been sleepy for an hour," Rachel admitted.

Stacey looked at her travel alarm and groaned. "It's only nine-thirty and there's nothing to do but go to sleep."

Rachel exchanged a look with Linda and Terry. All three of them were half-annoyed, half-amused. *There's always one in the group*, the look seemed to say.

Yawning, Rachel undressed and pulled on a long-sleeved flannel shirt, then slid into her sleeping bag. After the others were ready, Linda reached up and pulled the string on the light, and the cabin was instantly dark. The four of them chatted for a few minutes, about school and boys mostly, and then the cabin was quiet.

When Rachel woke up a while later, it was still quiet. Still dark. So dark, she finally knew what it meant not to be able to see her hand in front of her face. What time was it? Probably two or three, she decided. She lay still and listened.

No birds. It was too late. Or too early. She could hear the others' breathing, soft and rhythmic. She could hear the wind outside, up in the tops of the trees. It was strange, how you could stand beneath them and see that the wind was blowing but not be able to feel it.

Suddenly Rachel stiffened. She'd heard something else, something that didn't belong in a secluded mountain camp in the middle of the night. She lay completely still. Her heart was making more noise than anything else, but even above the beating, she could hear the other sound.

A twig snapped. Then another. Gravel rustled. Rachel imagined bears and racoons, but they wouldn't be so steady, would they? The sounds she heard were quieter, more deliberate. Like someone walking.

Then she thought of Mr. Drummond.

He'd scared her earlier. But he worked for the camp, he was here to protect it. That's probably what he was doing right now. Walking around again, making sure everything was all right. He probably did it two or three times during the night, making the rounds like a guard or something.

She heard more twigs, more rustling gravel. She wondered if he'd flash his light over the cabin, the way he had earlier. What had he been looking for, anyway? Fire, animals, holes in the roof?

Rachel waited, eyes wide in the dark, but no flashlight beam appeared. Then she realized that the noise outside had stopped. She could hear the wind again, and the breathing of the others. She could still hear her heart thumping in her ears, but it wasn't as loud. Mr. Drummond was gone.

Gradually, her eyelids got heavy. She yawned and turned on her side. She'd tell the others in the morning. Stacey would love it — she'd probably insist on figuring out a way to bar the door. Rachel smiled at the thought and snuggled deeper into her sleeping bag.

But just as she was about to drift off to sleep, she thought of something: the way Mr. Drummond walked. Solid, heavy, not caring how much noise he made. The sounds she'd heard were softer and quieter. They were footsteps, she was sure of it. But they didn't belong to the groundskeeper.

Someone else had been outside the cabin.

Chapter 4

Did anyone hear me? I had to be outside, just for a little while. I had to walk, and think, and tell myself I was really here. But did they hear me? Did they lie in the dark, listening, trying not to scream? If they heard me, they kept quiet. But when I closed my eyes, I could hear them. In my mind, I could hear them scream. I could imagine how it will be.

But now is too soon. I'll have to be more careful. It's not time yet. When I'm ready, when I start, I'll hear them scream for real. I'll never have to imagine it again.

Rachel stared at herself in the mirror of the shower cabin and frowned. Her green eyes had gray smudges under them this morning. Her light brown hair, which usually curled by itself if there was any humidity, now hung straight and limp in the dry mountain air. It wasn't long enough to tie back, either. She should have had it cut really short before she came.

She blinked and turned away from the mirror. She always looked bad in the morning, so what was the big deal?

The big deal was those footsteps she'd heard in the middle of the night.

She'd tried staying awake, wondering if they'd come back. But she must have been closer to sleep than she thought, because the next thing she knew, it was morning. Everyone else was gone, and there was a note from Terry saying they'd see her at the lodge for breakfast.

Now she closed her eyes and remembered the steps again. Lightweight and quiet. Not Mr. Drummond. Unless he tiptoed. Who, then? Tim or Michelle? She supposed one of them could have taken a walk. Or maybe somebody from the cabin had. She'd heard their breathing, but the cabin was so dark it was impossible to know if everyone was there. But then she remembered that the cabin door squeaked. She was sure she would have heard it if someone had gone out.

Suddenly, her eyes snapped open.

Of course. It was probably one of the guys. Or all of them, planning some kind of trick. They were all supposedly young adults, most of them on their way to college, but this was camp. She remembered summer camp very well. The boys liked to scare the girls and hear them shriek. The guys were probably regressing.

Rachel shook her head and laughed. She'd have to warn the others later. Maybe they could come up with a trick of their own. A surprise attack.

Hanging her nightshirt on a hook, Rachel hurried, shivering, into one of the shower stalls. She hadn't wanted to shower at the lodge, not with everyone else already there and wide-awake, so she'd decided to use the shower cabin. It wasn't as bad as Stacey'd said, but it wasn't exactly luxurious. The water pressure was almost nonexistent, and the water itself was barely lukewarm. One of Stacey's famous spiders had built its web across an upper corner, but spiders didn't bother Rachel much.

After her shower she dried off, still shivering, and pulled on jeans and a sweatshirt. Later, after the sun warmed everything up, she'd probably change. She toweled her hair dry, tugged a comb through it, and hurried across the grounds toward the lodge.

"Sleeping beauty!" Steve announced when Rachel walked in. "Better set that alarm from now on, Rache. When the campers get here, you'll have to be up before them."

"Don't pay any attention to him," Linda said, setting a plate of toast down on one of the tables. "He just got here himself."

"About thirty seconds ago, as a matter of fact," Jordan said.

"Traitors." Grinning, Steve reached for some toast.

The lodge's main room was big, with a fieldstone fireplace and thick beams timbering the ceiling. It was used as a dining hall when camp was in session, but now all but two of the wooden tables were shoved against the walls. The kitchen was across a wide hallway, and Rachel had smelled coffee as she passed by. She crossed the wide-planked floor and sat at one of the tables, across from Paul.

"I'm late because I woke up in the night and had trouble getting back to sleep," she said. She grinned back at Steve. If there was a plot to scare the girls, he was probably behind it. He seemed like the type, always teasing and poking fun. "You wouldn't happen to know why, would you?"

Steve munched on his toast and looked confused. "Why would I know something like that?"

Rachel almost laughed, but she decided not to say anything more about it right now.

"Never mind. I'm still groggy, I guess."

"Have some coffee," Linda suggested, coming back from the kitchen with another plate of toast. Behind her was Mark, carrying two coffeepots. It looked like Linda had organized breakfast duty. Rachel had thought it would be "serve yourself," but she didn't mind being waited on. The next day would probably be her turn in the kitchen.

"Did I hear you say you were up in the night?" Terry asked softly.

"Not up, just awake," Rachel said. She raised her eyebrows. "I'll tell you about it later."

Terry stared at her for a second, her dark eyes questioning. Then she nodded, as if she'd gotten it.

Rachel poured cornflakes into her bowl, took a piece of toast, and glanced around at the others. Stacey was taking small sips of orange juice, looking half-awake. Mark was drinking coffee and gazing off into the distance. His eyes were the palest of blue and his hair was white-blond. He didn't look much like a fun guy, although that's what Stacey had said. He looked remote and cold, as Rachel remembered from yesterday. But maybe he was just waking up, too.

Linda, of course, was wide-awake and bursting with energy, talking with Tim and Michelle about the plans for the day. Jordan and Terry and Paul were eating quietly. When Rachel reached for the milk, Paul caught her eye.

"Linda told me Mr. Drummond paid you a visit," he said.

Rachel nodded. "It was a little scary, after what Stacey'd said about him. But all he did was ask if everything was all right."

"And was it?"

"Sure." Rachel poured the milk onto her cereal. "I guess I should feel sorry for him. I mean, he's big and he has this deep, scary voice and everybody's afraid of him. I wonder if he knows it."

"Everybody's not afraid of him," Paul said. "I never was. Stacey likes to — " He stopped himself abruptly and shook his head. "You can't believe everything you hear."

Stacey likes to exaggerate, Rachel thought. That's what he was going to say. She looked at Paul and he smiled, as if he'd read her mind. The smile lit up his face, and his hazel eyes sparkled. Stacey'd said he was too serious, Rachel remembered. But maybe Stacey had never seen him smile like that.

After breakfast, they went to work. Linda

and Terry and Mark headed out to start cleaning cabins. Steve and Jordan and Paul went to check on the boats and the dock. Stacey was going to work in the "rainy-day building," as it was called, a building with Ping-Pong tables, Nok-Hockey boards, books, magazines, board games, and other things to help pass the time when the weather was bad. Rachel would much rather have been outside, even cleaning latrines, but last night she'd been assigned to set up the bulletin board in the lodge.

This was Camp Silverlake's twentieth anniversary, so they wanted Rachel to pick a bunch of photographs taken over the years and arrange them on the bulletin board. "Twenty Years of Summer Fun," or something like that.

Michelle and Tim helped her bring out boxes of photographs from the director's office and put them on one of the tables. Then they took the Jeep down to the closest town for some supplies.

At first, the photos all looked alike. Kids swimming and boating, playing softball, working on a crafts project. All of them suntanned and happy looking. One summer looked a lot like another.

But gradually, Rachel started to get into it, finding pictures that stood out from the rest. There was a great shot of a small girl on one of the hiking trails, wearing a backpack so huge and heavy she looked like she was ready to topple over backward. There was a dramatic shot of two kids scaling rocks, one of them reaching her hand down to the one below.

Then Rachel found a photograph of Mark. He was much younger, of course, probably about eleven or so. But it was definitely Mark. Even then, he had that cool stare and icy blond hair. He was standing a little to the side of a group of three other kids, and as Rachel looked more closely, she saw that they were Steve, Jordan, and Stacey. Stacey's hair was in pigtails, and she was twisting one of them around in her fingers. She was also wearing glasses. Steve's long face was red from laughing. Jordan was wearing a baseball glove and a small, mysterious smile. All three of them were looking at Mark.

Grinning, Rachel set the photograph in the pile she'd chosen for the bulletin board. It wasn't a great picture, but it was perfect, since the four of them were counselors now. She'd have to make a label for it. But for now, she'd just put it up and let them discover it for themselves.

Rachel decided to try to find a picture of Paul to put with it. As she was looking through the box from that summer, she found a photograph of another boy. He had shaggy brown hair and a big Band-Aid on his leg. His arms were hanging down at his sides, his skinny shoulders slumped a little. He was standing alone on the dock, staring out at the lake, and Rachel could see pine trees and clouds reflected in the water. Nobody else was around. It made her smile, but it made her a little sad at the same time. She didn't know why — the boy didn't look sad. He was just staring at the water. Ten seconds after the picture was taken, he had probably dived in, or turned around and made a silly face. Anyway, it was a beautiful picture. Rachel decided to make it the centerpiece of the bulletin board.

Cutting a frame for it out of blue construction paper, Rachel took it into the entranceway where the big bulletin board was attached to the wall. She'd just finished stapling it into the middle of the board when the door thudded behind her. Startled, she dropped the stapler and spun around.

He filled the doorway. A big man, tall and wide, with small eyes, a thick neck, and a gleaming bald head.

It couldn't be anybody else, Rachel thought. She hadn't seen him clearly, but she remembered him on the path last night, walking behind her out of the darkness. In spite of what

Paul had said about him, she felt her heart speed up and her mouth got a little dry. She swallowed. "Mr. Drummond," she said.

He stared at her for a moment. Then he nodded. "You're . . . ?"

"Oh." Rachel realized he was asking her name. "Rachel. Rachel Owens. I'm one of the counselors. I guess you probably figured that out."

He took a handkerchief out of the pocket of his jeans and ran it over his face and head. "Getting hot."

"I'll bet!" Rachel knew she was talking too loud, but she couldn't help it. The man made her nervous. Why couldn't the camp have a loveable groundskeeper, the kind who told funny stories and gave kids Popsicles?

Tucking the handkerchief away, Mr. Drummond took a couple of steps into the entrance. Rachel moved backward and almost tripped on the stapler. She bent down and picked it up, fiddling with it nervously. "I was just starting to fix up the bulletin board," she said, waving the stapler at the picture. "I found a lot of pictures of you. You won't mind if I put some of them up, will you? After all, you're as much a part of the camp as the lake, practically. I mean — I don't mean you're part of the scenery, but . . ."

Rachel's voice trailed off. Mr. Drummond wasn't listening anyway. He'd seen the photograph she'd put up. He walked over to it, his work boots pounding the wooden floor. Rachel watched as he bent slightly to get a better look. He stared at it for a long time.

Rachel didn't like the silence. "I'm going to be putting up lots of other pictures," she explained. "Some from every year since the camp's been in business. I thought that one was really special, though. It looks like something you'd see in an ad."

Straightening up, Mr. Drummond turned around.

Rachel stopped talking.

His eyes were narrowed and his face looked tense and angry. He'd been carrying a hammer when he came in, and Rachel could see his hand tighten on it.

She took a step backward.

"You've never been here," he said.

"What do you mean? Camp Silverlake?" Rachel shook her head. "No, this is the first time — I didn't go here when I was younger, if that's what you meant. Why?"

Mr. Drummond didn't answer, but his face relaxed a little. So did his grip on the hammer. He glanced over his shoulder at the picture again, then back at Rachel.

"It's good," he said, finally. "You couldn't have picked a better one."

He turned again and went into the kitchen. Rachel heard the water running. She moved through the archway into the main room. In a few seconds, the water was shut off and Mr. Drummond came back into the entrance hall.

He didn't look at the picture again. He didn't turn his head and look at Rachel. He strode through to the heavy front door, hauled it open, and went outside.

Rachel let her breath out, only just realizing that she'd been holding it for almost a minute. Her knees felt a little shaky. She looked over at the photograph, by itself in the middle of the bulletin board. What was wrong with that picture?

Suddenly Rachel had a thought. Maybe the kid in the picture had made Mr. Drummond feel bad. Acting scared (probably not acting, though), screaming and giggling whenever the big man walked by. Kids could be mean that way.

Except, why would Mr. Drummond say she couldn't have picked a better picture? It didn't make sense, not if the boy had been mean to him. And why had he wanted to know if she'd ever been there before? That didn't make sense, either.

Frowning, Rachel carried the stapler back to the table and sat down. Maybe Mr. Drummond hadn't meant anything. Or maybe whatever he meant was perfectly clear to him and he just had trouble communicating. Stacey said he never talked. She'd exaggerated about that, too. But Mr. Drummond was obviously a man of few words. He could be shy, Rachel thought, or just a loner.

Whatever he was, she decided to steer clear of him. Paul must be made of iron if that guy had never scared him.

Thinking of Paul made Rachel remember what she'd been about to do before she'd found the other photograph. She grabbed a handful of pictures from the same box and shuffled through them, looking for one of Paul.

She'd just found one — a shot of Paul cannonballing into the lake — when a piercing shriek shattered the silence of the lodge.

Chapter 5

Rachel jumped up so quickly, her chair tipped over and landed with a crash on the floor behind her. The sound echoed in the big room.

It was quiet outside now and Rachel listened, wondering if she'd imagined the scream. Or maybe it was some species of mountain bird she'd never heard of. Or a mountain lion. Were there mountain lions around here?

But the silence didn't last. The scream came again. Over and over, high-pitched and frantic. Rachel's skin prickled. Still clutching the photograph of Paul, she ran across the room and out the front door.

The screaming was coming from the lake. It was still going on, but not as loud, and the pauses between were longer. Rachel raced down a path, pine needles scattering under her feet, branches catching at her hair and the sleeves of her sweatshirt. As she burst out of the trees into the clearing, she saw Linda and Mark and Terry running just ahead of her. Rachel reached the beach a few seconds after they did. They clumped together, gasping, as the scream came again.

It was Stacey.

She was in the middle of the lake, floundering in the water and screaming every time her head bobbed up.

Not far from her was one of the rowboats. Steve and Jordan were in it, but they must have lost an oar. Jordan manned the other oar, while Steve paddled frantically with his hands, trying to get the boat to Stacey.

"My God," Terry said. "Why don't they jump out and swim to her?"

"She's not going to drown. She can swim — why's she so scared?" Mark asked, a note of irritation in his voice.

"She's panicked, Mark." Linda pulled off her shoes and started running toward the water, her hair streaming out behind her, coppery in the sunlight.

But just as Linda reached the shore, she stopped and looked off to her right. Rachel, who'd been following, looked too.

Paul was already halfway to Stacey in another boat, pulling the oars through the water in strong, even strokes.

"Come on, Paul," Rachel whispered.

Stacey was still bobbing up and down, slapping the water with her arms. When she saw Paul's boat, she screamed again, as if she were afraid he would pass her by. The boat glided up to her, and Rachel saw Paul unhook an oar and hold it out. Stacey grabbed hold of it with both hands, quiet now.

The water carried the sound of Paul's voice. Rachel couldn't tell what he was saying, but he was obviously talking to Stacey, calming her down. In a few moments, she let go of the oar and gripped the side of the boat. With Paul's help, she hoisted herself in, her feet slapping at the water.

Rachel and the others walked over to the dock and watched Paul row back. Behind him, still minus an oar, Steve and Jordan followed slowly.

The minute the boat bumped the dock, Stacey scrambled out, water streaming from her hair and dripping onto the boards under her bare feet. Rachel wondered if she'd lost her shoes in the lake, but now was hardly the time to ask.

Stacey was fine, but she was also furious.

"I'll kill him," she muttered through clenched teeth. "I will, I really will! I'll kill him!"

"Stacey, what happened?" Terry moved toward her and started to put an arm around her shoulder, but Stacey spun away from her.

"Just leave me alone, okay?"

"Come on, Stacey, relax," Mark said.

She glared at him. "I'm surprised you weren't part of it," she said. "Actually, you probably were. When did you cook it up — last night?"

Mark smiled, almost the first time Rachel had seen him do it. "You're kidding, right?"

Stacey didn't bother to answer. She turned back to the lake and watched Steve and Jordan making their way in.

Terry looked nervous and upset. Linda was watching the whole scene as if it were a movie, her eyes flicking back and forth between Mark and Stacey and the other boat.

Paul had climbed out of his boat by now, and Rachel went over to him while he tied up. "What happened?" she asked.

Paul stood up, rubbing his hands on his jeans. "Steve and Jordan went and asked her if she wanted to go out in the boat," he said quietly. "I guess she said yes, because I gave them a shove off and she wasn't complaining. The next thing I knew, she was screaming. Steve was standing up in the boat and he had Stacey in his arms, like a little kid. Then he tossed her overboard." He shook his head. "I thought they were just fooling around at first."

Terry had edged closer and was listening. "Is she scared of the water?" she asked quietly. "If she's scared of the water, why did she go out in the boat?"

Stacey whirled on them. "Because I'm not scared of boats!" she shouted at Terry, who shrank back. Just as quickly, she turned away, her hands bunched into fists.

Steve and Jordan had finally reached the dock. Paul took the line and tied it while they climbed out of the boat. Steve must have known what to expect, because as soon as he was on the dock, he put his hands up like a suspect with a gun pointed at him.

"Stace, Stace," he said, a smile tugging the corners of his mouth. "Sorry about that. Really, I am. I got carried away."

"Don't give me that!" Stacey shouted. "You didn't get carried away. You knew!"

"But Stacey, it's been what — six years?" Steve's lips moved as he counted silently. "No, seven. Seven years, Stacey. We've changed. We've grown up."

Mark chuckled. "Some of us have," he said snidely.

"Right." Stacey seemed to align herself with Mark. "Some of us have grown up, but not you,

Steve. You're still the same."

Jordan had been standing by quietly the whole time. But now it was his turn. "And you," Stacey said, rounding on him. "You just sat there and kept your mouth shut while he threw me in the lake. You're just the same. You haven't changed either."

Jordan stared down at the dock, his hands on his hips. He obviously didn't know what to say.

Rachel figured Steve had done this to Stacey before, when they were campers. She didn't blame Stacey for being upset, but she couldn't understand how Stacey could be a counselor if she was so frightened of the water.

Linda must have been wondering the same thing. "Stacey, I had to pass a lifesaving course to get this job. Didn't you?"

Stacey shook her head.

"I didn't either," Terry said. "Not all the counselors have to qualify in lifesaving, just a certain number."

"Right." Stacey took a deep breath and let it out. "Look," she said more calmly, "I can swim, okay? Not very well, maybe, but I can do it. I just don't do it if I don't have to." She looked out at the lake and shuddered. "I don't mind swimming pools at all. It's places like this, where you can't see the bottom. I feel like I'm being sucked down, and I get so scared I forget what to do. Don't tell Tim or Michelle about this," she added quickly. "They might tell the directors and I might get fired. My parents would absolutely freak."

"But what about when camp opens? Linda asked. "I mean, we'll all be taking kids out in the boats, won't we? You can't be in charge of kids in the water if you're scared of it yourself."

"Look, Linda, I'll figure out a way to get out of that," Stacey said. "I'm the arts and crafts counselor, anyway. They probably won't expect me to take kids swimming. Just don't tell anyone about this, okay?"

"I still don't understand why you went out in the boat in the first place," Terry said softly.

"Because I wanted to," Stacey said impatiently. "I already told you, I'm not scared of being on a boat. I know it doesn't make any sense, but that's the way it is."

Mark cleared his throat. "It doesn't have to make sense," he said, taking charge. He moved over to Stacey and put an arm around her shoulder. "But if you go out in a boat again, just remember to wear a life jacket."

"Yeah," Stacey said, shrugging off his arm angrily. "And I won't get in the same boat with Steve again."

"Come on, Stace," Steve pleaded, pretending to pout. "Give me another chance."

Stacey frowned at him. "You'd better be nice to me, Steve, or I'll tell everybody what *you're* scared of."

"Uh-oh," Jordan said. "Look out, Steve, she's playing dirty."

Stacey laughed, but Rachel could tell she wasn't amused. "Snakes," she announced. "Steve's scared of snakes."

"I'm not exactly crazy about them myself," Linda said.

"But I mean *really* scared. Like he freaks out. Remember, Jordan?" Stacey said, a sly smile spreading across her face.

Jordan looked at Steve. "Yeah, I remember. We were climbing rocks one day and there was this rattlesnake up there, too, minding its own business."

"Ha," Steve said. "It was lying in wait, planning an ambush."

"One of the counselors had to take Steve back to camp," Stacey said haughtily. "He almost fainted."

"Okay, okay," Steve said. "You win, Stacey. I confess. I have this problem with the slimy things."

"They're not slimy," Mark corrected him. "For your information, that's called a phobia."

"Whatever it is, I've got it," Steve said, gritting his teeth. "Are you happy, Stacey? You've humiliated me in front of everybody. Are we even?"

"I guess so." Stacey said, but there was still a glint of anger in her eyes. "We're even for now, anyway."

Saying she was going to change into dry clothes, Stacey headed for the cabin. After a few moments of tense silence the others started to scatter, getting back to what they'd been doing before the interruption.

Turning to go to the lodge, Rachel saw Mr. Drummond, standing at the end of a path, watching them all. He must have heard the screaming and come to see what had happened. Now, he turned away and walked back into the shadows of the trees.

Walking toward another path, Rachel heard someone behind her and turned to see Jordan, hurrying to catch up with her. "Hi," she said. "Are you giving up on boats for a while?"

"No, I just wanted to talk to you for a second." He stopped beside her and shoved his hands in his pockets.

Rachel waited.

"It's about what happened to Stacey," he said. "I forgot how she is about the lake. Steve was teasing her, threatening to throw her in, and she was laughing. Well, she was laughing until he actually did throw her in. I didn't think she was really scared."

"How come you're telling me and not Stacey?"

"Hey, I'll tell her. I just didn't want you to get the wrong impression." Jordan reached out and tucked a strand of Rachel's hair behind her ear. "I guess I don't want you to think I'm a bad guy."

"Okay." Rachel smiled, but she wasn't sure how she felt. Jordan was cute, and he seemed nice, but she couldn't help wondering why he hadn't apologized to Stacey first. But maybe she was being too hard on him. Stacey hadn't been in much of a mood to be apologized to. "Okay," she said again. "You're not a bad guy. I never thought you were."

Jordan smiled. He had a dimple in his left cheek. "Great."

Rachel's hair had slipped from behind her ear, and as she reached up to tuck it back, he took her hand. "What's this?"

"What?" Rachel looked and realized she was still holding the picture of Paul. It was a little creased from being clutched so tightly. "Never mind," she said, smoothing it out and tucking it in her jeans' pocket. "You'll see it later."

"Come on, what's the secret?"

She shook her head. "It'll be a surprise. For

some of you, anyway." Laughing, she started walking backward, away from him. "Something you probably don't want to be reminded of. Be prepared for a blast from the past."

Jordan had been laughing, too, but now he stopped and stared at her. "What did you say?"

"I said . . . I don't know, what *did* I say?" Rachel asked, confused by his attitude.

"About the past. What were you talking about?" Jordan demanded.

Rachel couldn't figure it out. What was he getting so intense about?

"It's no big deal," she said. She slid the picture out and showed it to him. "Here, see? It's Paul, when he was a camper. I found another picture of you and Stacey and Steve and Mark, and I'm putting them on the bulletin board. A blast from the past. Get it?"

Jordan shifted uneasily. "Why wouldn't we want to be reminded of that?"

"I just meant the way you guys looked," Rachel explained. "Not that you looked bad or anything. But I'm always kind of embarrassed when I see pictures of myself when I was little."

"You mean we looked like a bunch of geeks." He was smiling again, his dimple showing.

"Well, I wouldn't go that far," Rachel said. "But anyway, what's the problem? What did you think I was talking about?"

He shrugged and pushed his hair off his forehead. "I don't know. Nothing, really. Hey, listen," he added, "I'd better get back to work."

"Okay." Just like last night, Rachel stood there a minute and watched him.

Something strange was going on with Jordan. He wasn't just moody the way some people were. He was moody for a definite reason. She had no idea what it was, but she did know something was wrong.

Stacey was scared of the water, and Steve panicked at the sight of a snake. Jordan was scared of something, too. But what?

Chapter 6

By lunchtime, Rachel had almost finished the bulletin board. It had been kind of fun arranging the pictures, labeled by years, around that central photograph of the boy on the dock. She'd kept an ear out for Mr. Drummond's heavy tread, but he hadn't come back to the lodge, and neither had anyone else.

Fooling with the bulletin board had taken her mind off the scene with Stacey, but she couldn't shake the strange feeling she had about Jordan. One minute he was flirting with her and the next he was acting like he couldn't wait to get away from her.

Rachel didn't know what she'd said to make him change. All she'd talked about were the pictures from the past. She liked him; she just wished he'd come right out and tell her what was on his mind. Then maybe she could decide whether she liked him enough to flirt back.

She kind of wished Paul was the one who was doing the flirting. But except for that single fabulous smile, he wasn't acting very friendly, to her or anyone else.

As Rachel was stapling a few more pictures to the board, the front door opened and Tim and Michelle came in. "Hey, that looks good," Tim said, peering at the board over the top of a grocery sack. "The directors are going to love it."

They both laughed when Rachel pointed out the pictures of Paul and the other four when they'd been campers. "It's great," Michelle agreed, smiling at Rachel. "Everything okay while we were gone?"

"Sure. Fine." Rachel had decided not to tell them about Stacey and the lake. Not yet, at least. Terry was right to be worried about Stacey being in charge of kids in the water, but Rachel figured Stacey would get out of it, like she said. If she didn't, then Rachel would talk to Stacey and make her tell them. It would be too late to fire her then, anyway.

Tim and Michelle had brought food for the ten of them for the rest of the week. Rachel helped them carry all the bags into the kitchen, and while they went to round up everyone for lunch, she started putting the stuff away. She was washing apples at the big stainless steel sink when she heard someone come in.

It was Linda.

"I'm glad it's you," Rachel said. "Mr. Drummond came in before and I got really spooked being in here alone with him."

"What did he do?"

"Nothing." Rachel suddenly remembered Mr. Drummond's reaction to the picture on the bulletin board. "Well, he acted kind of weird, but it didn't have anything to do with me."

"What do you mean?"

Rachel told her about the picture and Mr. Drummond's reaction. "I decided he's just not used to communicating," she said. "Hey, did you see the bulletin board?"

Linda shook her head.

"Well, go look at it," Rachel told her. "See if you can find Stacey on it. And Mark and Paul and Steve, too."

"You're kidding — when they were campers, you mean?"

Rachel nodded. "It'll give you a laugh. Go look at it and tell me what you think."

Linda grinned and left the kitchen. Rachel went back to the apples, drying them and putting them in a big wooden bowl along with some bananas. When she heard footsteps behind her, she thought it was Linda. "So, what did you think?" she asked, not turning around.

"Who was cuter then, Paul or Jordan?"

"Frankly, I think I was," Mark's voice said.

Surprised, Rachel turned from the counter. "Oh, hi. I thought it was Linda." A little embarrassed, she tore off a paper towel and wiped the counter. "I take it you saw the bulletin board."

"Yes." Mark's pale eyes were narrowed to slits. "Did you have a lot of fun with that, Rachel?"

Before Rachel could answer, Steve and the others came in. They were all strangely quiet. Stacey and Steve kept looking at Mark, as if waiting for some kind of cue. Jordan went straight to the refrigerator without even glancing at Rachel. Terry seemed uncomfortable, and Paul leaned against the door frame, watching them all as if they were on stage.

Rachel laughed nervously. "Well, geez, what's the matter? I put some old pictures of you guys up and you act like I've committed a crime."

She glanced at Terry. *Her* picture wasn't up there. Why was she upset?

"I think they're cute," Rachel went on, "but if you really hate them that much, I'll take them down."

Mark stared at her a second longer. Then he shifted his weight and seemed to relax. When he did, the others did too. Before Rachel could ask them why they'd reacted so strangely, Linda came bouncing back into the kitchen. "I love it, Rachel!" she said. "Mark, you look exactly the same. And Stacey, the glasses. I never knew you wore glasses."

"I don't anymore." Stacey fingered her blonde hair and made a face. "I hated those things. That was the last summer I wore them. From then on, it was contacts."

The others laughed, and then they started poking fun at the way they'd looked back then.

Only Paul hung back a little, still watching.

Rachel was confused. Nobody seemed to remember that when they first walked into the kitchen, the tension had been so strong it was practically visible. Now they were acting as if it had never happened.

But Rachel knew she hadn't imagined it. Now she felt that something was off, not just with Jordan, but with everyone who'd been at Camp Silverlake seven years ago.

Chapter 7

During lunch, everyone talked about what they should do with the rest of the day. Tim and Michelle said it was up to each of them — they could keep doing what they'd been doing or find something else. "As long as we get the camp ready for opening, it doesn't matter," Tim said.

"So why don't we hike around and check out some of the trails," Jordan suggested. "Then we can come back and swim."

"Why don't we swim first?" Mark looked at Stacey. "Oops, never mind," he added quickly, but Rachel was sure he'd brought up the idea intentionally.

Steve snickered.

"What are you laughing at?" Stacey said to him. "For all you know, we'll run into another snake."

While they argued back and forth about what

to do, Rachel ate her sandwich and listened. Hiking sounded good to her; she was restless and felt like a walk. But it didn't really matter. She had something else on her mind anyway. She turned to Terry, who was sitting next to her. "What happened before?" she asked quietly. "With the bulletin board, I mean. How come everybody acted like I'd put up dirty pictures or something?"

Terry shook her head and swallowed. "I couldn't figure it out, either. We all came in and saw it at the same time and they just stared at it like the pictures might leap off the wall and bite them. It was very weird." She sipped some of her soda. "Then they headed for the kitchen, like a pack."

"That's exactly how it felt when they came in," Rachel said. "Like they were ready to gang up on me." She paused. "You looked kind of upset with me yourself."

"I did?" Terry looked startled. "I just thought maybe you put the pictures up to embarrass the others. I know I was wrong," she added quickly.

Rachel told her to forget it. But as she finished her sandwich, she couldn't help feeling a little sorry for Terry. She always seemed so nervous and uncomfortable. Rachel wondered how she would be when the campers showed up.

While Terry and Rachel had been talking, the others had finally agreed on checking one of the trails. Mark griped a little — he wanted to stick with what he'd been doing, so it would get done — but since he was the only one, he decided to go along. They cleaned up the lunch stuff, put some cans of soda and juice into a couple of small knapsacks, and set off.

A main trail led away from the campground and into the thick of the forest, where it was cool and hushed. Sunlight filtered down through the branches, making lacy patterns on the carpet of pine needles. After about fifteen minutes on a narrow path, they came to a clearing. Standing next to Paul, Rachel could see two or three trails branching off in different directions.

"Do you remember any of this?" she asked him.

"Yeah," he said, looking slowly around. "It's a strange feeling."

Up ahead, Michelle had started off on one of the trails and the rest of them followed. The trail was wide enough for walking two abreast, and Rachel brought up the rear with Paul. "What made you decide to come back here as a counselor?" she asked. "Happy memories?"

He looked at her, his hazel eyes almost green that day, matching his shirt. "I came here two summers in a row when I was a kid," he said. "The first time was great."

"What about the second time?"

He thought a minute, as if he was choosing his words. "Not as good," he said.

"How come?" Rachel asked. "You looked pretty happy in the picture."

"What . . . oh, right, the one on the bulletin board," he said. "Yeah, I love the lake."

"Listen, what was the big deal about that bulletin board, anyway?" Rachel asked. "I didn't think a bunch of old pictures would get everybody so uptight."

Paul stopped walking and turned to her. "I wish I could tell you, Rachel."

He sounded sad, Rachel thought. What was going on? "Why can't you tell me?"

"Because I'm not sure."

"Not sure about what?" Rachel gave her head a shake and laughed a little. "I feel like you're talking in riddles. Is this a game or something?"

Paul slowed to a stop and looked around. Off to one side of the path was a log. The branches of the trees around it drooped low, making the log seem like it was inside a cave. Taking Rachel's hand, Paul walked over and ducked under the branches. Rachel followed and they sat down together. The rest of the group hadn't seen them stop, and Rachel could hear their voices getting fainter and fainter as they walked on.

Paul leaned forward, his elbows on his knees, and frowned down at his sneakers. Some pine needles had caught in the laces, and he picked them out and twisted them around in his fingers.

Rachel wished he'd hurry up and say what he wanted to say, but she could tell he was trying to work something out in his mind. She picked up a pinecone, so she'd have something to keep her hands busy, too. Then she made herself keep quiet and wait.

After a moment, Paul sat up straight. "A few minutes ago, you asked me about the second summer I spent here," he said. "I said it wasn't so great."

Rachel nodded.

"That was kind of an understatement," he said. "Oh, for a while it was really fun, just like the first time. It's a great camp — it's not as modern as some others, I guess. No swimming pool, no computers, no tennis courts. But it's more relaxed, I think. I mean, your day's not scheduled down to the last second. You get some time to yourself."

Rachel laughed a little, she couldn't help it. "You sound like you're trying to sell me on the place."

"I guess I do. Sorry about that." He smiled and tilted his head back, looking up at the network of branches above them. "Okay, where was I?"

Rachel didn't think he'd forgotten. He was just having trouble getting to the point. But she told him anyway. "You were about to explain why the second summer wasn't as good as the first."

"Right. Okay." He tilted his head back down and started fiddling with the pine needles again. "Well, something happened that second summer," he said. "I don't mean I got homesick or didn't pass my swimming test or anything like that. I mean something went wrong. And it was bad."

Rachel stayed quiet again. Whatever had happened, she knew Paul still thought about it, and she knew it still bothered him, maybe even haunted him.

Haunted was the right word for the way he looked now. His lean face was pale under its tan and his eyes stared off into the distance, at something Rachel couldn't see.

She didn't know what memory he'd pulled from that summer, but she started to dread hearing it.

Finally Paul looked over at her. "It was bad," he said again. "Somebody died. A boy. You put his picture right in the middle of the bulletin board."

Chapter 8

Rachel felt like the breath had been knocked out of her. She'd been ready to hear about death — what else could have made Paul so sad and haunted but the memory of a death? But to hear that she'd put the kid's picture right out for everyone to see and remember — no wonder they'd reacted so strangely when they'd seen it. They'd probably thought she was trying to remind them and bring it all back. Mr. Drummond must have thought that, too.

She thought of the boy in the picture and terrible images flashed into her mind — an accidental drowning, or a fatal fall from the rocks.

Rachel tossed the pinecone down and rubbed her arms. She was about to ask Paul what had happened, but before she got the words out, they heard footsteps pounding along the trail. She and Paul looked at each other and ducked out of their pine tree cave just in time to see Jordan running toward them.

"Hey, there you two are," he said. "What's going on?"

"Nothing." Rachel pointed to the log she and Paul had been sitting on. "We just took a break."

Jordan looked at the log, then back at Rachel and Paul. His eyes darkened, but he didn't say anything. Rachel knew what he was thinking, though — that the two of them had stopped to make out. She was a little annoyed. They'd been talking about death — not that it was any of Jordan's business — so how could they possibly look like they'd been making out?

"Why'd you come back?" Paul asked.

"Tim and Michelle. They got all worried," Jordan explained. "They thought you decided to go exploring or something and got lost."

"Well, we're fine," Rachel said. "Come on, let's catch up with the others." She took off along the path, leaving Jordan and Paul to follow. She wished Jordan hadn't interrupted them. She wanted to know what had happened that summer.

Jordan had been there then. He had to know. He had to remember. Stacey and Mark and Steve were there, too, and none of them had said a word. Why hadn't they bothered to explain it to her?

Rachel looked back at the two guys. They were walking together, not talking. She could ask now.

But Rachel didn't ask. She turned away and kept walking. It had been hard for Paul to talk about it, and it probably was for everyone else, too. Maybe they wanted to forget about it. Even Paul. After all, he hadn't mentioned it until she'd started asking questions. She decided not to say anything more to him. She'd wait for him to bring it up if he wanted to. She wouldn't say anything to anyone else, either. And she'd take the boy's picture off the bulletin board as soon as she got back to camp.

The group walked along the trail for about another twenty minutes, clearing away tree limbs that had fallen during the winter. The trail led through some dense forest, across an ice-cold stream, and into a clearing that had obviously been used before. Logs were arranged in a rough circle, and a pile of blackened rocks looked like the remains of a camp fire.

"Hey, I remember this place," Steve said, looking around. "We came up here one day and had a picnic."

"It's coming back to me, too," Mark said. He crossed to one of the logs and sat down. "Nature Walk Number One. Half-day. Leave camp in the morning, hike, eat, and be back in camp by early afternoon."

"Is that the way it works?" Terry asked. "You take a different trail depending on how long you want to be out?"

"Not really," Tim said. "All the trails run into each other at some point."

Stacey opened the knapsack she'd been carrying and handed out juice and soda. "I remember this place, too," she said, popping open a can of diet Coke. "If we keep going a little more, don't we come to a kind of lookout?"

"Hey, that's right," Jordan said. "It's like a platform, made of rocks, and you can look out over a valley for miles."

"This is the place," Michelle agreed.

"It sounds beautiful," Linda said. "Let's go see it."

"We *just* sat down," Mark pointed out lazily.

"You don't have to come," Linda told him.

"Yeah, Mark, stay here and commune with nature." Steve laughed. "We'll pick you up on our way back, unless a bear comes by before we do."

"Very funny," Mark stood up and drank the

last of his grapefruit juice. "Come on, let's get it over with and get back to camp. I want to go swimming."

Finishing their drinks, they put the empty cans back in the knapsacks and headed out of the clearing. Rachel wound up at the end of the line, walking behind Mark, and Paul was up front with Linda and Stacey.

Rachel had been hoping to walk with Paul again, not so she could talk to him about the boy who'd died, but because she liked him. He was kind of serious, but that didn't bother her. She knew he had a sense of humor, it was just buried kind of deep.

Or maybe being back at Camp Silverlake, remembering what had happened, had made him sad. She wondered why he'd come back. If he ever talked to her about it again, she'd ask him.

She couldn't stop thinking about the boy who'd died. When she'd applied for the job, no one had mentioned it. But she guessed they wouldn't. An accidental death wasn't something a summer camp advertised. Besides, it had been a long time ago.

Staring down at the trail, still thinking about the boy, Rachel almost bumped into Mark. He'd suddenly stopped walking and knelt down to re-tie his sneaker.

To keep from walking right into him, Rachel did a quick little side step to the edge of the trail. Looking around, she saw that it was just as Jordan described it — the trail had led up, out of the trees, and now she was standing in the open. The trail was about three feet wide here, and on both sides was a steep drop hundreds of feet down. Rachel was exhilarated; it was like being on top of the world.

"This is great!" she cried, spreading her arms wide.

"Mmm." Mark was busy with his shoelace and didn't look up. "The rock platform's not far. Just follow the trail."

Looking ahead, Rachel could see that the trail curved out of sight. She couldn't see the others, but she could hear them. They were shouting loudly, calling out their own names and listening for the echoes.

She started to walk ahead, then turned back, expecting to see Mark right behind her. But he was still busy with the shoelace. "What is it, a knot?" she asked.

"Yeah."

"I'm good with knots. Getting them undone, I mean. You want me to do it?"

"No, go ahead." Mark sounded frustrated. His usual smooth self-assurance was gone and his breath was coming fast as his fingers fumbled with the lace. "Go on, I'll be there in a second."

"Well, don't get all tied up in knots over it, ha-ha," Rachel joked. "Let me do it." She started back to him.

Mark raised his head and looked at her. His pale eyes weren't pale anymore. The pupils had widened until his eyes were almost black. His face was almost as white as his hair, and he was breathing even faster.

"What is it?" Rachel asked, worried. "Are you sick? You want me to call the others?"

Mark shook his head and gulped in some air.

"You look like you're going to faint," Rachel said. "I'm getting the others."

"No!" Mark stood up, swaying a little.

"But you're dizzy!" Rachel cried. "You might fall and get hurt!"

Mark grabbed her shoulder and steadied himself. "I'm fine," he insisted. "I'm okay. Will you just get going, Rachel? Just go on and get away from me!"

Rachel winced as his fingers bore painfully into her shoulder. It made her mad enough to go, but she really was afraid to leave him there, looking so sick. What could have happened?

He'd been all right ten minutes ago.

Slowly, Mark let go of her and eased himself back down until he was hunched over his sneaker again. Rachel stepped away and looked at him. His shoelace wasn't knotted at all. It wasn't even untied.

He'd made it up.

Suddenly, Rachel understood.

Mark was afraid of heights.

She should have guessed — her mother was the same way. Elevators and airplanes didn't bother her. She could be thousands of feet up, and as long as there were walls or something around her, everything was okay. But she couldn't even climb to the roof of their house without getting dizzy and breathless. Just like Mark.

And he was embarrassed about it. It was ridiculous, Rachel thought. So what if heights bothered him? There was no contest going on to see who was the bravest.

Rachel hesitated, still not sure whether or not to leave. Finally, she decided to go ahead. The trail wasn't so narrow that he could fall off.

"Okay," she told him. "I'm leaving."

"And not a moment too soon," he said sarcastically.

Rachel felt her face flush. "Well, if you plan to stay here, Mark, you ought to come up with a better excuse than that shoelace. It didn't fool me and it won't fool anybody else, either."

Rachel was never sure whether Mark had walked back to the clearing or crawled back, but that's where she and the others found him when they returned from the lookout. He was reclining on one of the logs, eyes closed, hands behind his head.

"What happened to you?" Jordan asked him. "You missed the lookout. It was fantastic."

Mark raised his head and yawned. His color was back, and his breathing was normal. "Too bad," he said. "I'll catch it another time."

He hadn't answered the question, but no one except Rachel seemed to realize it. She was still annoyed with him, and without thinking about it, she said, "How's the shoelace, Mark? Did you ever manage to get that knot out?"

The look in his eerie eyes was so deadly, Rachel felt like she'd been hit. She stepped backward, almost falling over another log. By the time she'd steadied herself, Mark was on his feet, walking away with Steve.

Rachel didn't think anyone else had noticed,

but as they started along the trail, heading back to camp, Terry said, "What was that about the shoelace? Mark looked like you'd spit on him or something."

"Mark always looks like he just smelled something bad," Stacey said.

"You said he was fun," Linda reminded her.

"He is, you just have to get to know him."

"I think I'll pass," Rachel said. "He acts so superior, and he is — a superior creep."

"So what was it with the shoelace?" Linda asked.

"He got scared on the trail out to the lookout and pretended he had a knot in his shoelace so he wouldn't have to keep going," Rachel said. "He's scared of heights, and he practically bit my head off when I asked if I could help."

Stacey laughed again. "We're great, aren't we? I'm scared of the lake, Mark's scared of heights, and Steve can't stand snakes. Maybe we should quit before the campers get here."

"Everybody's scared of something," Linda said. "With me, it's bees."

"Me too," Terry said. "Bees and bugs."

"What about you, Rachel?" Stacey asked. "What makes you squirm?"

"I get stage fright," Rachel said. "When I was in grade school, I always threw up whenever we put on a class play or anything like that. I can't stand lots of people staring at me."

On cue, the other three stopped walking and stared at her.

"Very funny," Rachel laughed. She felt much better. Mark hated her guts at the moment, but she wasn't going to worry about it. He'd probably get over it. "Listen," she said as they walked on, "I just remembered. I woke up in the middle of a sound sleep last night, and I'm pretty sure I heard someone walking around outside our cabin. Don't panic," she added, seeing the looks on their faces. "It definitely was not Mr. Drummond."

"What do you mean, don't panic?" Stacey said. "If it wasn't him, who was it?"

"That's exactly what I asked myself," Rachel said. "And I decided it was one of the guys. Maybe more than one, I couldn't tell. Anyway, I think they're up to something."

Terry looked worried. "What could they be up to? Why would they be walking around in the middle of the night?"

"I get it," Stacey said quickly. "You think they're planning to play a trick on us, right?"

Rachel nodded.

"I bet that's it," Linda agreed. "And Steve's probably in charge of it. He's just the type."

"Definitely," Stacey said. "Don't forget, I went to camp with him. I remember once when he — " she stopped and bit her lip, her cheeks reddening.

"When he what?" Terry asked.

"Oh, you know . . ." Stacey made a throwaway gesture. "He put pinecones in people's sleeping bags, stuff like that. Anyway," she went on quickly, "if they're planning a trick, what do you think it'll be, Rachel?"

"Something scary, I'm sure."

"Naturally," Linda said. "Weird noises or something. And then when we run out of our cabin, they'll throw water balloons at us."

Stacey laughed. "Let's make a bunch of water balloons ourselves, so we'll be ready."

"We could," Rachel agreed. "Or we could play our own trick, first."

"Ooh, I like that idea," Stacey said.

"Wait a minute." Linda stopped walking. "We're counselors now. We're supposed to be mature. This is extremely juvenile stuff we're talking about." She tried to look serious, but her amber eyes were sparkling. "I love it! What are we going to do?"

"I don't know, but whatever it is, it'll have to be tonight," Rachel said. "Otherwise they might beat us to it."

Stacey looked down the trail. The four guys were way ahead now, almost out of sight. "Tonight then," she said, turning back to the others with a wicked grin on her face. "Tonight is Fright Night."

Chapter 9

I always knew I would do something. It was a vow, a promise, and it got stronger and stronger as the years went by. But I was never sure exactly what to do. Even after so much time thinking about it, planning it, the most important part wasn't worked out. I came here not knowing. But now I know.

They made it so easy for me. They told me. Without realizing it, they showed me exactly what to do.

Now, I can start.

As they walked back to camp, they worked out the details of Fright Night. The whole thing was snowballing, turning into a complicated plan that involved weird noises, dark clothes, and wet leaves. The weird noises were supposed to make the guys come running out of their cabin. The dark clothes were so the girls wouldn't be seen. And the wet leaves were for stuffing into sleeping bags.

"They'll think they're slugs," Terry said. Rachel was surprised to see how much Terry was getting into the spirit — it seemed so unlike her.

"Or snakes," Stacey cackled. "I get to do Steve's sleeping bag. It'll *almost* pay him back for the lake."

"What should we do about our cabin?" Terry asked. "Once they figure out what we're up to, you know they're going to head right for it."

"One of us will have to stay there," Linda said. She'd taken charge, as usual. "Sort of like a sentry, to make sure they can't get in. Who wants to do that?"

"I will," Rachel volunteered. They were almot back now, and up ahead she could see the beginning of the campgrounds through the thick trees. "But listen," she added. "I think we're getting kind of carried away."

"Hey, it was your idea," Stacey said.

"I know. But I was thinking of something simple," Rachel said. "Like we'd make sure they were asleep and we'd make some loud noises and then run back to our cabin."

"As long as we're doing it, we might as well do it right," Linda said.

"I guess. It's turning into an awfully big production, though."

"That's what makes it fun," Linda insisted.

"Yeah, come on, Rachel. Don't spoil it," Stacey said.

"I'm not going to spoil it," Rachel said. "I just . . . oh, never mind. Forget I said anything."

The others went back to talking about the plan, and Rachel walked behind them, wishing she'd never thought of doing anything in the first place.

She wasn't sure why; that was the problem. It was just a feeling she had.

A feeling that Fright Night wasn't going to be any fun at all.

Once they reached the camp, everyone split up. Mark went swimming, which was what he'd wanted to do in the first place. Steve joined him, and Stacey waded around in the shallow water near the shore. Paul took a boat out alone and disappeared around a wedge of land that jutted out into the lake. Terry and Jordan volunteered for supper duty, and Linda got a drink in the lodge and then went back to the cabin.

Rachel had planned to take the boy's picture

down from the bulletin board, but she didn't want anyone to see her or to make a big thing out of it. She decided to get up early in the morning and remove the picture then, before anyone else came to the lodge.

She would have enjoyed a swim, but she didn't feel like being anywhere near Mark at the moment. Finally, she decided to go back to the cabin.

It was hot inside. Linda had changed into shorts and a tank top, and pulled her hair up into a knot on the top of her head. She was stretched out barefoot on her cot, reading a letter.

"You got mail already?" Rachel said. "How'd you manage that? Oh, wait, I bet I know," she went on. "Your boyfriend wrote you before you even left, right? This must be some romance."

"Mmm," Linda said, still reading.

"So what does he say?" Rachel asked. "How's his job? Does he miss you like mad? Oops, I forgot." She laughed again. "How could he miss you? He wrote the letter before you even left. Well, does he at least say he misses you?"

Linda looked up from the letter. "Yeah," she said. "He says it. It makes me want to see him so much. I wish he were here, right now."

"Boy, you've really got it bad," Rachel said. "Maybe you shouldn't have come here."

Linda shook her head. "Enough about Dan," she said firmly. "What about you?"

"What about me?"

"You and Jordan," Linda said. "Or you and Paul. Or you and both of them."

"Forget that," Rachel laughed. "Anyway, I didn't come here to find a boyfriend."

"Maybe not, but it would be kind of fun, wouldn't it?"

"I guess so."

Linda grinned. "So which one do you like better?"

"Paul, I think," Rachel said slowly. "Except I'm not sure how he feels about me. Especially after what he told me." She pulled off her sweatshirt and rummaged in her bag for a short-sleeved T-shirt. "You know the picture of that boy I put in the middle of the bulletin board?" she asked, tugging the T-shirt over her head. "The one standing on the dock, looking at the lake? Paul told me he died, right here at camp."

"*Died?*" Linda was quiet for a few seconds. Then she said, "How?"

"He didn't get a chance to tell me that." Rachel found a pair of shorts and started taking off her jeans. "I felt awful, though. Well, because he died, naturally. But also, Paul and the others were here at the same time, so they knew him. Or they probably knew who he was, at least. I guess they don't want to be reminded, because they haven't talked about it. Then I go and put his picture up and bring it all back."

"It wasn't your fault," Linda said. "You didn't know."

"No, but I'm still going to take the picture down," Rachel said, putting on the shorts. "Anyway, that's the longest conversation Paul and I have had. Actually, it's about the only conversation we've had. Not exactly romantic, huh?"

"Did he act mad?"

Rachel shook her head.

"Then everything's okay. Hey, I just got an idea." Linda stood up. "One of us wears a sheet tonight and pretends to be his ghost."

"What?"

"The boy's ghost, the one who died," Linda said.

Rachel stared at her. Was she serious? "I think it's a lousy idea," she said. "A kid died here, and those guys knew him, and you want to make a joke out of it?"

The smile disappeared. "You're right," Linda said quietly. "It was a lousy idea. I don't know why I even thought of it." She tucked a strand of hair back up into the knot and sat down again. "We'll stick to the original plan. Wet leaves in the sleeping bags. No ghosts."

"Right. No ghosts." As Rachel stuffed her dirty clothes into her laundry bag, the picture of the dead boy flashed into her mind.

Was that what had made her sad when she first saw the picture? Did she somehow know, or feel, that she was looking at someone who died? She shivered in the hot cabin.

"No ghosts," Rachel said again.

By the time dinner was over, Rachel was in a much better mood. Jordan and Terry had made spaghetti and salad, and everyone ate like horses and joked about how the food wouldn't be as good once the campers arrived. Mark seemed to have forgotten that he was mad at her. At least he didn't give her any more evil looks. Paul was in great spirits, and banged out some songs on the old upright piano in the lodge's main room. He wasn't very good, but he laughed when they teased him and said that they couldn't even carry a tune, so what were they griping about? Rachel found herself liking him more and more.

"You look more awake tonight," Jordan said. He was standing next to Rachel, so close she could feel his skin brush her arm whenever he shifted his weight.

"I am," Rachel agreed. The rest of the group was singing an off-key rendition of "You Are My Sunshine," and she almost had to shout. "It would be impossible to sleep with this going on. But it's fun. I'm having a great time. It's like we're all finally getting to know each other."

Jordan leaned closer. "Want to take a walk?"

"Why?"

He laughed, so softly she couldn't really hear him. "Give me a break, okay? I could have said, 'Want to take a walk so we can get to know each other even better?' but I thought it sounded a little too obvious."

Rachel felt herself blush. She was almost ready for college, but she was still a social klutz. "Sorry."

"Nothing to be sorry about." Jordan took her hand. "Let's go."

"We're really having a communication problem," Rachel laughed. "I meant, sorry, I don't want to take a walk. I'm having a good time in here."

Jordan glanced over at Paul. When he looked back at Rachel, his blue eyes had darkened, like they had earlier when he'd found them together on the trail.

For a second, Rachel thought he was going to argue, or say something nasty.

Finally, though, he just moved away from her. She watched him walk over to Terry, bending close to her ear, talking and smiling. She wondered what he'd do when Terry told him about her boyfriend. Would he move on to Linda? And then to Stacey?

He sure didn't have any trouble changing directions, Rachel thought. Stacey had called him wishy-washy. It wasn't quite the same thing, but Rachel knew what she meant. He seemed to check which way the wind was blowing before he decided which way to go. She wondered if there was anything he'd be willing to buck the wind for.

Like the night before, everyone headed back to the cabins about nine-thirty. But Stacey didn't complain about it this time. Before dinner, she'd gone into the woods and filled a garbage bag with a mess of sodden, decaying leaves and now she couldn't wait to put their plan into action. They had to wait, though, until they were sure everyone was in for the night. Finally, a little before midnight, they started getting ready.

"I just have one question," Stacey said as she pulled on jeans and a black sweatshirt. "What do we do if we run into Drummond while we're out there?"

"Enlist him," Linda said.

"Are you kidding?" Stacey said. "He'd probably report us."

"Big deal." Linda tucked some strands of bright red hair up into a navy-blue baseball cap. "Stacey, you act like you're still ten and you could get in trouble. Tim and Michelle won't care about this, so forget about Mr. Drummond."

"He came into the lodge while Jordan and I were fixing dinner," Terry said. "Did you know he has a room there?"

"From the way Stacey talks, I thought he probably slept in a cave," Linda said.

Terry shook her head. "Anyway, I kind of told him he might hear some strange noises tonight and not to worry."

"What?" Stacey looked annoyed. "Now he'll definitely be out there. Lurking." She flopped down on her cot. "Either that or he'll warn the guys. Did Jordan hear you tell him?"

"No, he was setting the tables," Terry said. "Look, I thought Mr. Drummond ought to know. I was afraid of what he might do if he didn't know."

"Oh. Well, maybe you're right," Stacey said. "I just hope he doesn't rat on us."

"I don't think he will," Rachel said. "I don't

think he says anything unless he has to."

"You're right," Terry agreed. "When I told him, he didn't say a word. He just stared at me for a second and then he left." She shivered. "He's a very strange man."

"No kidding." Stacey twisted her hair up and pulled on a dark baseball cap like Linda's. "Well. Are we ready?"

Rachel looked at them and laughed. They were in jeans, dark sweatshirts and caps, and since all their shoes were white, they'd decided not to wear them. Instead, they'd each put on several pairs of dark socks. "You look like a bunch of cat burglars," she said.

"That's the point," Stacey said, her eyes gleaming. "We move through the night, silent and invisible."

Linda turned to the others and whispered, "Let's go."

Stacey picked up the bag of leaves, and the three of them left the cabin, telling each other to be quiet and trying not to laugh.

Rachel shut the door behind them and latched it. She wasn't supposed to open it unless she heard the coded knock — three short taps, a pause, then one more tap. Turning from the door, she pulled the light string, then felt her way in the darkness to her cot and sat down. She heard a couple of muffled giggles outside the cabin, and the rustle of the garbage bag. Then there was silence.

Lying down on the cot, Rachel closed her eyes and pictured their progress. The plan was for them to get to the guys' cabin and make thumping noises on the sides of it. This was supposed to bring them out. Linda and Terry would let themselves be seen for just a second, and then run off into the woods. While the guys followed, Stacey would rush into the cabin and stuff the sleeping bags. She'd meet up with Linda and Terry at the girls' shower cabin and they'd come back here together.

None of this was supposed to take very long. The whole point was for them to get back there and pretend to be awakened when the guys started shouting about the leaves in their sleeping bags. Rachel figured if everything went smoothly, Terry, Linda, and Stacey should be back in about fifteen or twenty minutes.

Sitting up, she pulled back the shade on the window and looked outside. Naturally, she couldn't see a thing. She shut her eyes again and listened. The guys' cabin wasn't that close — down one of the paths and through a patch of trees — but she thought she might be able to hear the thumping. She wasn't sure Stacey would be able to keep from laughing, and she thought she might hear that, too.

All she heard was the wind.

But they'd only just left. It was too soon to hear anything. Rachel stayed by the screen, listening and waiting.

A few more minutes passed. Rachel's foot went to sleep. She stood up and shook it until the prickling went away. Then she felt her way across the cabin and fumbled on one of the shelves for Stacey's travel alarm. Its hands glowed green in the dark. It was fifteen minutes past midnight. They'd been gone for at least twenty minutes.

Rachel took the alarm clock with her and sat back down under the window. She still couldn't hear anything. She told herself it was just taking longer than they thought it would. Maybe the guys had caught up with Terry and Linda. Or maybe Stacey had been caught in the cabin. But if that had happened, wouldn't she hear them shouting and laughing?

Rachel let five more minutes go by, and then she made up her mind. She'd go see what was happening. This was taking too long. If she ruined the trick, too bad. They could get mad if they wanted to, but she wasn't going to sit here alone any longer.

She stood up and moved to the center of the cabin, waving her hands around for the light string. She kept missing it and finally she gave up. Terry had a flashlight, and so did Linda, but Rachel didn't feel like searching for them. She wanted to get out. The dark was like a blanket, close and heavy. It was dark outside, too, but at least she'd be able to breathe out there. She moved to the door, her hands out in front of her, and felt around for the hook.

She found it and was just about ready to slide it up when she heard someone on the other side of the door.

Chapter 10

Relieved, Rachel started to slide the hook all the way out. Then her fingers froze. Whoever was out there hadn't given the coded knock: three short, pause, one more. Maybe she was being silly, but sitting alone in the dark cabin had hardly been relaxing. She felt jittery and nervous; if she opened the door and it was someone playing a trick, she knew she'd scream loud enough to bring Tim and Michelle, who'd think she was being murdered. She held her breath and waited for the knock.

It didn't come.

Rachel leaned her head against the door and waited some more. Nothing happened. All she could hear now was her own breathing, and the wind high up in the trees. Had she just imagined that somebody was out there? She thought she'd heard movement, a shuffling sound, like someone trying to walk quietly. Sneaking up.

But now she heard nothing.

Okay. This was getting ridiculous. So she'd open the door and somebody would leap at her and scare her half to death. So what? At least she wouldn't be standing in the dark like an idiot, sweating and listening to her heart beat.

Silently, Rachel slid the hook up and out. She found the door handle, took a deep breath, and quickly pulled the door all the way open.

The doorway was empty. The night was still quiet. Letting her breath out, Rachel cocked her head and listened. No hurried footsteps moving around the corner of the cabin. No whispery giggles.

Cautiously, she stepped out of the doorway and looked back and forth. Nothing. Nobody.

Still cautious, Rachel left the door open and tiptoed to the corner of the cabin. She peered around. When she didn't see anyone or hear anything, she walked the length of the cabin, around the end, along the other side, and back to the door.

She was the only one out here. She must have been hearing things earlier. Or imagining things. Nobody else was around.

Rachel started to go back inside, but then she stopped. The others had been gone for at least half an hour. Where were they? And why couldn't she hear anything? It was as if they'd left the cabin and walked off the edge of the earth.

Enough of this, Rachel thought. Fright Night had gone on too long. Leaving the cabin door open, she took off down the path. She didn't know what everyone else was up to, but she was going to find them. She didn't want to be alone anymore.

There was still no moon, and Rachel stumbled a few times on pinecones and roots, and walked into a couple of low branches. But by the time she reached the girls' shower cabin, her eyes had adjusted to the dark.

The light in the shower cabin was off. Rachel found the door and went inside. She couldn't find the light string in here, either. For a moment, she stood on the gritty cement floor and listened, wondering if anyone was hiding in the shower stalls. All she could hear again was the sound of her own breathing.

Back outside, into the cool night air. Shivering, rubbing the goosebumps on her bare arms, Rachel peered down the path in the direction of the guys' cabins. There were six of them, but the guys were staying together in one, like the girls were. She couldn't see any of the cabins yet; they were farther along the path and behind a big stand of pines. But if their light was on, wouldn't she be able to see it shining through the trees?

She couldn't see anything, she couldn't hear anything. Where was everybody?

Rachel took a few tentative steps along the path leading toward the boys' cabins. Then she stopped.

She'd heard something.

A rustling in the trees over to her left. Her heart speeded up as she tried to see what had made the sound. A racoon? Mr. Drummond? A bear? Oh, God, not a bear. Not Mr. Drummond, either. She didn't know which would be worse.

The rustling sound came again. Rachel tried to convince herself it was something harmless, a bird or a squirrel. She tried telling herself that if it was a person, all she had to do was call out and the game would be up. But her body wasn't listening, her feet were already moving. Before she even thought about what she was doing, she'd run halfway back to her cabin.

Let them laugh, she thought. Let them congratulate themselves on scaring her out of her mind. She didn't care.

She just wanted this night to be over.

Wanting to look behind her but not daring

to, Rachel hurried up the path, pushing branches out of her way. They made a whipping sound as they closed behind her. If anyone was following, they'd get a face full of pine needles, which was fine with her.

Scared and mad, Rachel raced toward the cabin. As she got close, she saw that the door was still standing open and the light was still off. No way was she going to run into that gaping black hole and let everyone jump at her. She'd go to the lodge, that's what she'd do. She'd get something to drink and wait in the lodge until everyone started worrying about what had happened to her. Then they'd come looking for her and the whole rotten joke would be ruined.

Without slowing down, Rachel turned away from the cabin and ran back along the path, this time toward the lodge. Now she could hear the water, lapping at the shores of the lake. In a few more seconds she'd be out of the trees, in the open, and she could run like mad without bumping into anything.

Just as Rachel burst out of the trees, a dark shape loomed up in front of her.

She was moving too fast to stop, breathing too hard to do anything but let out a feeble gasp. She tried to swerve, but it was too late.

She ran headlong into the shapeless figure, colliding with it so hard the breath was knocked out of her.

She heard someone else's breath whoosh out, felt someone's hands on her arms. She was still struggling to get away when she realized he was saying her name.

"Rachel! Rachel, come on, cut it out!"

It was Paul.

Rachel pulled away from him and bent over, hands on her knees. Her legs were shaking, her arms were shaking, she was gasping for breath. In a moment, she felt his hand on her back.

"What's going on?" he asked. "Are you all right?"

Still bent over, Rachel turned her head and glared up at him. "What kind of question is that?" she snapped. "Do I look all right?"

Paul shifted his weight but he didn't take his hand away. "Well, no. But forget I asked that. What I really want to know is what's wrong?"

Rachel's breathing was almost back to normal now. She hadn't run that far, she'd been gasping out of fear more than anything. She straightened up and faced him. "I got scared," she said. "You really don't know why?"

"Why would I ask if I knew?" Paul stuffed his hands in the pockets of his jeans and shook his head. "You come barreling out of the woods and nearly run me over and then you act like I should know what's the matter. Come on, Rachel, is this a game?"

"That's what *I* want to know." Rachel looked toward the lodge and saw light coming from some of the windows. "Is that where you were? At the lodge?"

He nodded. "I got hungry."

"You ate two plates of spaghetti," she said skeptically. "I saw you. Full plates."

"I wanted something sweet, so I ate some cookies and . . . geez, Rachel! What is this?"

Rachel was still suspicious. "Where's everybody else? Are they at the lodge, too?"

Paul must have decided he wouldn't get any answers until he gave some of his own, because he didn't argue. "Let's see," he said seriously. "All of us — all of us guys, I mean — went there, about midnight, maybe a little before."

Just about the time Linda and the others left our cabin, Rachel thought.

"Mark left the lodge first, then Jordan and Steve," Paul went on. "I was the last one to go."

"Who's over there now?"

Paul looked back at the lodge. "Well, Tim and Michelle. And Mr. Drummond, I guess. But I didn't see him."

"That's all?" Rachel was starting to get skeptical again. "And how come I didn't see Mark or Jordan or Steve? I've been outside for fifteen minutes at least."

"Um, there's more than one path back to the cabins," Paul reminded her. "Maybe they took a different one."

"What about Linda? And Stacey and Terry?"

"What about them?"

"You mean they weren't at the lodge?" Rachel asked. "You haven't seen them?"

"Rachel." Paul put his hands on her shoulders and bent his face close to hers. "I promise, you're the only girl I've seen out here tonight."

If it had been any other time, Rachel might have enjoyed the feeling of his hands and the closeness of his face. But she was too worried to appreciate the situation. "Then where are they?" she said. "They left at midnight, too, and they haven't come back. Where are they?"

Paul started to say something, probably ask her what she was talking about again. But then his gaze shifted, and he looked past her shoulder into the trees.

Rachel spun around and looked, too. At first she didn't see anything. But she could hear the sounds. Not bears or raccoons. People, definitely. She heard voices and laughter, and then she was able to see who it was.

It was everyone. Stacey and Terry and Linda, still dressed in their dark clothes. Steve and Mark and Jordan, laughing and teasing as they prodded the girls forward.

"Look who we found wandering around in the woods!" Steve cried when he saw Paul and Rachel. "Forest elves!"

"Woodland sprites," Mark said.

Jordan laughed and held up the garbage bag Stacey had filled with wet leaves. "It was a plot," he said. "They were going to sabotage our cabin."

Rachel looked at Paul, feeling a little foolish. "I guess you can figure it out," she said.

"I think I have an idea." He smiled and nudged her. "What's in the bag?"

"Wet leaves. For your sleeping bags," Rachel admitted. "But something went wrong, I guess."

"Aww. Too bad," he laughed, nudging her again.

Rachel laughed, too.

But she couldn't help wondering what had gone wrong. And where Stacey and Linda and Terry had been all this time.

Steve and Jordan couldn't resist opening the garbage bag and pelting everyone with clumps of wet leaves. But after a lot of good-natured insults, the group finally split up and headed for their cabins. The minute the guys were out of sight, Rachel asked what had happened.

"It's no big deal," Stacey said, as they walked back up the path. "We were almost to their cabin when we heard them coming out. So we ran."

"I thought for sure they'd hear us," Terry said. "But they didn't even look."

"I still don't get it," Rachel said. "Didn't you run together?"

"No, we weren't sure where they were going," Linda told her. "Once I saw they were heading for the lodge, I doubled back, but I couldn't find Stacey or Terry."

"I was in the woods. Look at me." Terry held out her arms. "I'm covered with pine needles. A big branch reached out and ripped my cap off and I think I've got sap in my hair."

"I ran into the shower cabin," Stacey said.

"But I looked in there," Rachel said. "It was empty."

"The *boys'* shower cabin."

"Oh."

"Anyway, I walked around a while looking for Terry and Stacey, but I was afraid to call out," Linda said. "So I just sat down and waited."

"Didn't you hear me?" Rachel asked. "Didn't anybody hear me?"

"I guess not," Stacey said. "I thought I heard something, but I was getting kind of scared. It was creepy out there."

"No kidding." Rachel felt a pinecone crunch under her foot. "Then what happened? How'd they find you?"

"I guess we all decided to go looking for each other at the same time," Terry said. "We just met up when the guys came down the path and saw us."

"I guess we blew it," Linda sighed. "They'll be expecting something now, and we won't be able to trick them."

"Yeah, they'll probably try something on us, too," Stacey said.

Rachel didn't care. She was glad the whole thing was over. All she wanted now was to go to sleep.

When they reached their cabin, Terry stopped. "The door's open," she whispered.

"Of course it's open," Rachel said. "I left it open. When I was running around in the dark, alone, looking for you guys, remember?"

"But they might have been here." Stacey was whispering, too. "While we were all out, they could have snuck in and done something."

Rachel was tired of the whispering and the tricks. "How could they?" she asked loudly. "They were all at the lodge, remember? We were the only ones running around tonight."

"What's the matter, Rachel?" Linda pulled off her baseball cap and her silky hair rippled onto her shoulders. "You sound upset."

"I'm not upset!" Rachel heard herself almost shouting. "Okay, okay, I am upset. A little. I just got nervous before when I couldn't find you."

Linda smiled and patted Rachel's shoulder. "Well, we're all here now. And we're all okay. Let's go in and go to sleep."

Rachel was the first one into the cabin. She walked in with her arms up, waving her hands in the air for the light string. This time, she was lucky. She felt the string brush her fingers, and she managed to snag it on the first try.

She yanked the string and the light came on.

At exactly the same time, a howl of fear splintered the air around them.

Chapter 11

Rachel's fingers were still around the string, and the howl startled her so badly she jerked it again, plunging the cabin into darkness.

"Turn it on!" Stacey cried. "Turn the light on!"

The string had slipped from her fingers. Rachel frantically felt for it in the air.

The hoarse scream came again.

"What *is* that?" Terry gasped.

"*Who*, not What." Linda's voice was cracked. "*Who* is it?"

"Turn the light on!" Stacey cried again.

"I'm trying!" Finally, Rachel felt the string again, got hold of it, and pulled the light on. The four of them looked fearfully at each other, eyes blinking in the glare.

"An animal." Terry's voice shook. "It was an animal."

"I don't think so." Linda looked toward the open door. "I think it was one of the guys."

"A joke?" Stacey asked hopefully. "Maybe it's a joke and they're trying to scare us?"

"If it is, it worked." Terry took a deep breath and let it out. She started to smile, but then her face froze as the awful cry tore through the night again.

Rachel looked around and grabbed a flashlight. "Come on," she said. "It's coming from their cabin and it's not a joke. Somebody's hurt."

"I don't want to go out there!" Stacey protested.

"Rachel's right," Linda said, picking up another flashlight. "We have to go see if we can help."

Rachel was already out the door, with Linda just behind her. Terry followed, and Stacey, too nervous to be left alone, ran after them.

It was scarier with the flashlight, Rachel thought as she ran along the path toward the other cabins. The little beam made the dark seem darker and the shadows bigger. Linda was almost on her heels and their flashlight beams bobbed together as they ran.

The terrible cry didn't come again, but as they got closer to the other cabins, Rachel could hear someone gasping hoarsely, almost sobbing.

Then she heard Paul's voice.

"Stay still! Just try to stay still!"

"I can't! I don't think I can!" Steve's voice, high-pitched now. Whining with fear.

It was Steve who had screamed, Rachel thought.

"God," Linda breathed behind her, "what could it be?"

"I've got a stick," Jordan's voice said.

"Don't be stupid." Mark's voice, harsh and arrogant. But scared, too. "You might miss."

The cabin door was open, light spilling out. Just before they reached it, Rachel and Linda slowed to a walk. Terry and Stacey caught up to them as Rachel stepped closer to the door.

Mark and Jordan were just inside the doorway, their backs against the walls. Jordan had a stick in his hands, gripping it tightly. Paul was a little farther in, standing very still. He seemed to sense the girls moving into the doorway; he slowly turned his head and looked at Rachel.

Rachel stopped, her hand on the door frame. Behind her, Linda whispered, "What? What is it?"

Rachel put her hand back to stop her, but

Linda pushed up next to her anyway.

Steve was in the middle of the cabin, sitting on the floor. About two feet away from him, its rattle quaking an ominous warning, was a coiled rattlesnake.

Chapter 12

Not far from the snake was a sleeping bag, still partially rolled up. It was lying in a heap, as if it had been flung to the floor. The snake must have been inside it, Rachel thought. Steve probably started to unroll the bag, then screamed and threw it on the floor when he saw the snake.

Sweat was pouring down Steve's face into his eyes and mouth, but he didn't dare move to wipe it away.

His fear was so powerful, Rachel could almost feel it.

Anyone would have been scared. But for Steve, it was much worse. He'd laughed when Stacey teased him about snakes, but it was obviously no joke. He was terrified, whimpering, crying.

It was horrible to watch, and Rachel looked away. "Somebody go get Michelle and Tim," she said. "And Mr. Drummond. Stacey, go get them. They must not have heard anything, so go get them. Tell them what's happening. Tell them to hurry."

"I can't see anything," Stacey said. "I don't know what's happening."

Steve started gasping. "You sure about that, Stace?"

"There was a rattlesnake in his sleeping bag," Linda said. "Stop complaining about the view, Stacey, and go get help."

Terry and Stacey took off.

The snake's head bobbed and its rattle quivered. Its tongue shot out of its mouth, searching.

Steve gasped again. He was sitting, bracing himself with quivering arms. "I can't . . ." he sobbed. "I can't . . . stand this!"

"Hang on, Steve," Paul said softly. "Somebody's coming."

"Looks like the gang's already here," Mark said.

Rachel shot him a look. He was really a creep.

"Could we try to get the sleeping bag?" Linda asked. "Maybe we could throw it over the snake."

"That'll never work," Mark said. "The snake's too close to it."

"Right," Jordan agreed quickly. "We shouldn't move."

"The others'll bring a shovel or something," Paul said. "Just hang in there, Steve."

Steve didn't answer. His whole face was a mask of fear, glistening with sweat and tears.

The snake's head waved again, low to the floor. Its rattle quivered like a tiny castanet. Its tongue slithered out and in like a devil's fork.

Steve whined again, a steady, rhythmic whine, low-pitched at first, then getting higher and higher. Rachel wanted to tell him to stop — she couldn't stand the sound. It made her want to scream, too.

Then she heard something else — footsteps pounding toward the cabin. Heavy footsteps, running fast. Rachel knew who it was before she even turned her head to look.

Carrying a square-headed shovel, Mr. Drummond ran toward the cabin door. Rachel and Linda stepped aside and let him in. He stopped for only a moment, his face impassive as he looked at the snake and the crying boy.

"Stay still," he murmured. He took a step into the cabin, a lighter step than Rachel thought possible. Then he raised the shovel in both hands like a spear, lunged, and brought its metal edge crashing down. The snake was cut in half.

No one moved, except Mr. Drummond. The shovel was imbedded in the wooden floor, and he tugged it out, then scooped the snake into it.

He turned toward the door, his small eyes glittering as he looked at everyone for a moment. Rachel thought his lips curved up in a tiny, secret smile. But it was gone so fast she wasn't really sure if she'd seen it or imagined it. Then, without a word, he left the cabin.

Still, no one moved. No one spoke. Steve seemed frozen, his hands braced behind him, his face still glistening. Rachel closed her eyes and let her breath out. Behind her, she heard Tim and Michelle talking softly, coming toward the door.

Before they reached it, Steve was on his feet. He seemed to have shot up in a second. Now his long face was a mask of rage, ugly and menacing. "Stacey!" he shouted. He hurled himself toward the door, knocking Rachel aside. *"Stacey!"*

"What? *What?*" Stacey sounded annoyed, but when she saw Steve's face, her expression changed to fear. "What are you — "

Before Stacey could finish, Steve was on her. Grabbing her by the arms, he started shaking her and shouting. "Are you happy now? Huh? You happy now?"

Stacey tried to struggle, but Steve had her arms in an iron grip. He shook her so hard her head whipped backward and forward and her mouth opened and shut like a marionette's. "You think that was funny?" he shouted. "You turned me into a blubbering jerk! Are you happy now?"

Everyone had been stunned motionless for a few seconds, but suddenly they came alive. Tim and Michelle took hold of Steve and started pulling at him, but he was so furious they couldn't budge him. Mark and Jordan ran up and grabbed his arms, tugging and yelling at him to cool off. Linda put her arms around Stacey's waist and tried to pull her away from him.

Finally, Steve let go of Stacey by himself. Giving her one last shake, he flung her away from him like a rag doll. The others let go of him, and he stood alone, his chest heaving.

Stacey recovered quickly. Rubbing her arms, she glared at Steve. "You're crazy!" she shouted at him. "If you think I put that snake in there then you're crazy!" She took a step toward him, brought her arm back, and slugged him on the shoulder with her fist. "You jerk! How could you think I'd do anything like that?"

Steve just looked at her.

Mark cleared his throat. "Well, Stacey, you were pretty mad at him for throwing you in the lake. And tonight, you were out roaming around with a garbage bag."

"Full of *leaves*!" Stacey yelled. "You saw it!"

"Yes, well, I saw *that* bag," Mark agreed. "Anyway, you have to admit, you've been known to play a trick or two on people."

Stacey narrowed her eyes. "So have you, Mark," she said. "We all have. Just don't forget that."

A faint smile flitted across Mark's lips.

"Listen," Michelle said, "this isn't doing anybody any good. I don't blame you for being upset, Steve, but you have to know that Stacey — that nobody — put that snake in there."

Steve stared at the ground and didn't say anything. His anger had vanished. He looked embarrassed, Rachel thought. Humiliated because everyone had seen him crying in panic.

Rachel glanced at Paul, who was standing near her. He was still watching Steve and the others, his expression curious, thoughtful.

Linda was watching them, too; her face was pale.

Jordan stood with his hands resting lightly on his hips. His head was down, but he glanced up from underneath his eyebrows, his gaze flickering nervously over the others' faces.

Terry was leaning against a tree. Her dark eyes were wide and staring into the distance. Rachel looked away, but then her eyes returned to Terry's face. It seemed Terry's lips were curved into a small, private smile.

Finally, Steve took a deep, shuddering breath and straightened his shoulders. "Stace," he said softly. "I'm sorry. I freaked out."

"Yeah. Well. Okay." Stacey shifted her weight and nodded. "Okay," she said again.

Mark yawned loudly. Jordan grinned.

Tim clapped his hands together. "All right. What do you say we call it a night?"

Nobody argued. Everyone shuffled around, murmuring goodnight, and then the girls started back along the path. Rachel looked back once. Paul was still standing in the doorway in a pool of light, watching Mark and Jordan and Steve as they filed into the cabin.

No one spoke as they were walking back. Rachel figured that if they felt anything like she did, they were too tired to talk. It wasn't the time, it was the tension. She felt wrung out and drained, and a dull throb had started behind her eyes.

In the cabin, Stacey made a beeline for her

cot. Yanking the sleeping bag off, she flapped it up and down in the air. Nobody asked her why. In fact, they all did the same thing. Then they searched under the beds and on the shelves, prodded their duffel bags and checked in all the corners. Satisfied that there weren't any snakes, they sat crosslegged on their cots and looked at each other.

Stacey broke the silence. "I can't believe Steve thought I'd do something like that," she said. "I mean, I wouldn't turn into a babbling idiot if I saw a snake around here, but I sure wouldn't get close enough to one to put it in his sleeping bag."

"He didn't mean it. He said so," Linda reminded her. "He was hysterical."

"Hysterical is right," Stacey said. She sounded angry and disgusted.

"You know how he felt," Terry told her. "You're the same way about the lake."

"Yeah," Stacey said grudgingly. "But why didn't he just run?"

"He was afraid it would strike if he moved," Rachel said. "I guess it all happened too fast for him to think. It was awful seeing him like that. You could tell he was embarrassed about it."

"He was afraid we'd laugh at him," Terry

said. "And I bet he thinks we'll tease him about it tomorrow."

Terry's little smile was back, Rachel noticed. Was she hoping Steve would get teased? Would she enjoy it?

Mark probably will tease him, Rachel thought. Stacey might, too, if she was still mad enough. Rachel wasn't crazy about Steve, but she couldn't help feeling a little sorry for him. He needed better friends. "I don't think we should say anything about it unless he does," she said. "We have to try to act like nothing happened."

"Yeah, well something *did* happen," Stacey said. "I wonder if it really was an accident."

"What do you mean?" Rachel asked. "Who'd do something like that?"

Stacey lay back and stared at the ceiling. "Drummond, maybe."

"Oh, come on." Rachel started undressing. "He killed the snake. Why would he put it there if all he was going to do was come back and kill it?"

Stacey shrugged. "I don't know, except he's weird. Anyway, it was awfully convenient that the snake just happened to pick Steve's sleeping bag. The one person who turns into jelly when he sees one."

"You've got a point," Linda said.

Rachel pulled on her nightshirt and stared at them. She'd never thought the snake in Steve's sleeping bag was anything but a terrible coincidence. She'd never thought Mr. Drummond, or Stacey, or anyone, had put it there.

But what if someone had?

Chapter 13

Oh, it was beautiful. More than I'd hoped for, better than I'd dreamed.

When I heard the scream, I knew my plan was working. I've imagined that scream for years. Long lonely years. To finally hear it, really hear it, made it all worthwhile.

They think it's over. But it's just getting started.

Rachel was sure she'd wake up during the night. She was sure she'd have nightmares. But if she'd had any, she couldn't remember them. And when she woke and looked at the clock, she saw that she'd slept straight through to the morning. Daylight brightened the dark window shades, and she could hear birds outside, fluttering in the branches of the trees and calling to each other.

It was nine-thirty. Linda and Stacey were

already gone, and Terry was sitting up and stretching.

"I can't believe it," Terry said with a yawn. "I thought I'd have snake dreams."

"Me too." Rachel unzipped her sleeping bag and swung her feet to the floor. "I hope nobody else did."

Terry looked at Rachel. "I can't help wondering about what Stacey said. About Mr. Drummond."

"You mean whether he put the snake there?" Rachel stood up quickly, feeling angry. She didn't like hearing her own thoughts put into words. "I don't believe that. I can't believe it. Just because the man's kind of strange doesn't make him a maniac. And anybody who'd do something like that would have to be crazy."

"Maybe." Terry got up and reached for her robe. "Maybe not. But you don't have to get so mad about it."

"Sorry." Rachel sighed. "Anyway, what did you mean, 'maybe not'?"

"I just meant a person doesn't have to be crazy to play a nasty trick." Terry belted her robe and picked up the little bag where she kept her shampoo and toothpaste. "But never mind. You're probably right. I was just wondering, that's all." Smiling, she left the cabin.

Rachel sighed again. She wished Terry

hadn't said anything. She didn't want to be thinking about something like that first thing in the morning.

Why had Stacey even mentioned Mr. Drummond? If anyone had a reason to put a snake in Steve's sleeping bag, Stacey did.

But no one did it. *No one.*

Rachel washed quickly, then got dressed and walked over to the lodge to eat. She'd meant to get up early, too, and take down the boy's photograph. Maybe she still would, if she could do it without anyone making it into a big deal.

"Rachel, hi. Wait up."

Turning, Rachel saw Paul coming toward her through the trees. His dark hair was damp and there were comb tracks running through it. "I see you just got up, too," she said when he'd caught up to her.

"Mmm. We were all a little wiped out."

"How's Steve?" Rachel asked. "Is he okay?"

"I guess so. He's not making many jokes this morning, though." Paul frowned and shook his head. "I think he thinks everybody's going to make fun of him for the way he reacted last night."

Rachel nodded. "Terry said that, too. But he shouldn't be ashamed."

"No," Paul agreed. "But he's not used to being on this side of things."

"You mean he's the one who usually does the laughing," Rachel said.

"And the tricks."

"But this wasn't a trick." Rachel frowned. "Wait, you're not thinking it was, are you? Stacey's got this idea that it was Mr. Drummond, but I don't believe it. Nobody would do anything so dangerous, would they?"

"I don't know. Somebody might." Paul stopped walking and looked at her. His eyes now looked blue-gray above the blue of his shirt. "You can't be sure what somebody might do."

Rachel wanted to ask him what he meant, but they'd reached the lodge and Terry was coming out, with Linda behind her. Terry had obviously showered at the lodge. She was still in her robe and her hair was wet. "I forgot to bring my clothes with me," she said, scooting past them.

Linda stopped for a moment. "Stacey and Mark fixed scrambled eggs," she told them. "Jordan's eating them all, so you'd better hurry. See you later."

When Linda left, Rachel turned to Paul again. But out of the corner of her eye, she saw Steve coming toward the lodge. Now was not the time to talk about snakes or tricks or anything like that. She'd have to talk to Paul again, though. If he thought it was done on purpose, who did he think did it?

Steve didn't say much at breakfast. Everyone else talked a blue streak about everything but what was really on their minds. They were trying too hard, Rachel thought. They should just talk about it and get it out in the open. But she didn't do it herself, so she guessed she couldn't expect anyone else to do it either. She kept sneaking looks at Steve. He seemed nervous and edgy, as if he expected someone to crack a joke at his expense. What a change, she thought.

The plan for the day was to clean all the cabins. Then they'd take the boats out, row to the other side of the lake and have a picnic. Late lunch or early supper, depending on what time they left. "When we get back," Tim said, "you're free."

"Free to do what?" Stacey asked.

"Free to collapse." Steve looked around, a ghost of his old grin on his face. "When we get back, we'll be too wiped out to do anything else."

It wasn't that funny, but everyone laughed, glad to have him joking again.

Rachel volunteered to clean up the breakfast stuff. She hated to cook, but she'd never minded washing dishes. Besides, she wanted to stay behind by herself and take the photograph from the bulletin board. She got busy carrying trays of plates and cups into the kitchen, keeping an eye out until everyone left.

Finally, the lodge was empty. Well, maybe. She hadn't seen Mr. Drummond this morning, but she figured she'd hear him before she saw him anyway. She stacked the last few plates in the sink and ran water over them. Then, drying her hands on a paper towel, she went into the office where the boxes of pictures were stored.

After a quick search, she picked out a photograph of a freckle-faced girl standing next to the Camp Silverlake sign at the entrance to the camp; she took the picture and the stapler out to the bulletin board.

Rachel hadn't looked at the bulletin board when she came in for breakfast, but now she stopped and stared. The picture of the boy was gone. The blue construction paper frame was there, but it was empty, framing nothing but light-brown cork.

Rachel looked on the floor to see if the picture had fallen somehow. It wasn't there. Of course it wasn't. How could it have fallen when it was stapled up?

Someone had taken the picture down. Someone who didn't like what it reminded them of.

It had to be somebody who'd been here that summer, Rachel thought. One of the other counselors. Or Mr. Drummond. She wondered if it was Paul. The memory of that death really disturbed him.

But if Paul had taken the picture, wouldn't he have told her? She liked to think he would, because she had the feeling that something was starting between them.

Maybe she was wrong about that.

Well. She wished whoever took it had said something to her. But it didn't matter, she guessed. She'd been planning to take it down anyway.

Slipping the new photograph into the paper frame, Rachel stapled it and then stepped back for a look. She didn't like it as well, but at least this picture wouldn't make anyone unhappy.

She was just about to take the stapler back to the office when something else on the bulletin board caught her eye. From where she was standing, it looked like one of the pictures had a smudge of dirt on it. She moved in for a closer look, and when she saw what it was, her scalp prickled and her heart knocked hard against her chest.

It wasn't dirt.

It was three concentric circles, drawn with

black Magic Marker. The circles were around Steve's face. All it needed was a cross in the middle. Then it would be like looking through the sight of a rifle, as if Steve's face were the bull's-eye of a target.

"You're being awfully quiet, Rachel." Mark pulled at the oars and gave her a sly smile. "Don't tell me *you're* scared of the lake, too."

Rachel shook her head. They were on their way to the other side of the lake, and she still wasn't sure how she'd managed to end up in a boat with Mark. But there was nothing she could do about it now. "I love the water," she said. "Lakes, swimming pools, anything."

"I just thought from the way you kept looking around, not saying anything, you might be nervous," he said, sounding as if the idea appealed to him.

Rachel *was* nervous, but not because of the water. It was because of the circles she'd seen on the photograph of Steve. She couldn't stop wondering who had drawn them, and why. Was someone trying to call attention to what had happened that night before — to humiliate Steve? Who?

Stacey came to mind immediately. She'd been furious with Steve for dumping her in the water. Then again, Rachel realized, it didn't have to be her. There seemed to be all kinds of secrets and tension between the group of old friends. For all she knew, it could have been any of them.

The sun was in Mark's face, and he took a pair of dark sunglasses from his shirt pocket and put them on. "Ah, much better."

It wasn't much better for Rachel, though. The glasses hid his eyes completely. She hated not being able to see somebody's eyes when she was talking to them.

"Well, if the water doesn't bother you," Mark went on, "what does?"

"Plenty of things," Rachel said. "But nothing special."

"You mean nothing that would turn you into a quivering mass of fear."

"Nothing so far," she said. She looked away at the other boats, hoping he'd take the hint and stop asking questions. What was he getting at? Did he want to know what frightened her so he could pay her back for seeing him so scared up on the trail?

So he could draw a target around her face?

Of course he couldn't do that — *her* picture wasn't up on the bulletin board. But he could have drawn the circles on Steve's picture. He definitely seemed like the type who would enjoy making fun of someone else's weaknesses.

Then Rachel remembered Terry's satisfied smile when she'd talked about Steve getting teased. She was always so nervous, except when they were planning the trick on the guys. Did she get pleasure out of seeing *others* scared for a change? Had she drawn the circles?

Rachel knew she was just avoiding thinking about what really was bothering her. It wasn't just what someone had done to Steve's picture. It was the snake. Maybe Stacey and Paul and Terry were right. Maybe someone did deliberately put the snake in Steve's sleeping bag.

If so, then that person was playing a game that could turn deadly.

Mark wanted to know what scared her. Well *that* scared her.

Chapter 14

There was no dock on the far side of the lake. Once they'd rowed to it, they dragged most of the boats up onto the rocky shore. There wasn't room for all of them, but Paul pointed out the wedge of land he'd rowed around the day before. It was full of jagged rocks, but it was shady and cool. They tied the last two boats to a massive, weathered log and left them there.

The day was cloudless and hot, and after they'd taken care of the boats, all anyone wanted to do was cool off. They'd all worn swimsuits under their clothes, and now they ran into the water, shouting and splashing each other. Stacey sat down in the shallow part near the shore and let the cool water wash over her.

Rachel swam hard, hoping the exercise would drive the image of Steve's circled face out of her mind. It didn't go away, but after almost an hour of swimming, she was too tired to try to make sense of it. She was starving, too.

They devoured sandwiches and fruit and cookies, and then Tim and Michelle got in one of the boats and headed back to camp. They had paperwork to do and some calls to make. After they'd gone, Linda wanted to take a walk. "It's much wilder on this side of the lake," she said. "I wonder if there are any trails."

"If there aren't, you can blaze one," Mark said.

"Not without help," Linda said. "Come on, let's go exploring."

Everyone was stuffed, but they slowly emptied sand from their sneakers and got up. Only Stacey stayed where she was, stretched out on a beach towel in the sun. "You guys can blaze trails," she said sleepily. "I'm staying right here."

"You're going to turn into a lobster," Mark warned.

"You could lie in one of those boats over by that log," Paul suggested. "It's shady there."

"Yeah, maybe. Anyway, I've got sunscreen on, don't worry." Stacey yawned and closed her eyes. "Wake me when you get back."

As Rachel took off with the rest of the group, she hoped they wouldn't run into any snakes. Steve must have been thinking the same thing, because after a few minutes of walking, she saw him split off in a different direction, one that would keep him closer to the shore.

Almost everyone split up after a while. There were trails, but they were so tangled with undergrowth, it was hard to keep up with the person ahead. Rachel could hear Linda laughing as she plunged in front of everyone else. She heard Jordan and Terry off somewhere to her right, but she couldn't see them. She had no idea where Mark was, which was fine with her. She was a little surprised he'd come. But maybe he knew that there weren't any high places around here.

She didn't know where Paul was, either. He hadn't started out anywhere near her. But now, when she turned to look, she caught a glimpse of his blue shirt through the thick trees. "Paul," she called. "Come on. Everyone's disappearing on us."

Pushing branches and vines out of his way, Paul caught up to her. "You're right," he said, after he'd listened for a moment. "I can't hear anyone now. I think we've been deserted." He reached out and pulled a twig from her hair. "Actually, I'm not sure I want to keep going anyway."

"Me either," Rachel laughed.

Paul looked around. They weren't in a clearing exactly, but there was some space. "Let's sit down for a while and then go back," he said. "Is that okay?"

"Sure." Rachel kicked away some deadwood and made a space next to a tree. They sat down together and leaned against the trunk. Wherever the others were, Rachel couldn't hear them.

For a few minutes, she and Paul talked about college. Rachel was going to the state university. Paul was going to a private college just a few miles away from it. "I don't suppose there's any chance we might run into each other," he said.

"I guess there's always a chance," Rachel said.

"Or we could make the chance." Paul smiled at her, that dazzling smile that changed his face.

Rachel's heart started thumping in a nice way; she thought a kiss was coming. It might have, too, if a sudden rustling in the trees hadn't made them both jump. Rachel's heart was still racing, but not from pleasure anymore.

After a minute, Paul said, "Probably a squirrel."

"Mmm." Rachel was still looking around. "I ought to be used to noises by now, but I'm not."

Paul nodded. "I think we're all a little jumpy after last night."

"I guess so," Rachel said. She closed her eyes and remembered Steve's face, terrified and covered with sweat. Then she saw his face in the picture, circled like a target. She snapped her eyes open.

Paul was watching her. "What is it? What are you thinking about?"

Rachel waited a second, and then she told him. "It's about Steve," she said. "I keep wondering if that snake crawled into his sleeping bag by itself. I'm afraid somebody put it there. Somebody who wanted to make him suffer."

Chapter 15

Paul just kept watching her. No more dazzling smile, of course. He didn't say anything, so Rachel took a deep breath and went on. "When Stacey talked about Mr. Drummond putting the snake there, I didn't pay much attention," she said. "I thought she was just . . . well, you know how she is."

"I know how she is," Paul agreed.

"Even when you said something about how we couldn't know what people might do, I thought you were wrong," Rachel told him. "You were talking about tricks, and I really didn't believe anyone would play a trick like that."

Paul sat forward, staring out at the undergrowth. "What changed your mind?"

"Steve's picture," Rachel said. "The one from when you guys were campers here. The one I put on the bulletin board. Did you look at it this morning?"

He shook his head.

"His face was circled." Rachel felt a little shiver of fear again. "It made him look like a target. And he was. If somebody put the snake in his sleeping bag, then Steve was their target." She leaned forward, too, wrapping her arms around her knees. "I guess usually you'd circle the target first and then do something, but that would be like a warning. This way there was no warning."

Paul was quiet, thinking about it.

"There was another thing," Rachel went on. "Except I don't think it had anything to do with Steve. You didn't look at the bulletin board, so you didn't notice, but the picture of the boy you told me about — the boy who died? — his picture was gone this morning."

Paul's eyes narrowed. "I wonder why."

"Well, so did I at first," Rachel said. "I was going to take it down myself, because I figured nobody wanted to be reminded of what happened. So I decided whoever took it did it for the same reason." She picked up a twig and turned it over in her fingers. "You never got to finish telling me about it. Do you mind?"

"No, not really." Paul sat back against the

tree trunk again. "His name was Johnny," he said. "Johnny Danard. Right away, some of the kids got to calling him Johnny the Nerd, instead. That's how it started."

"How what started?"

"The teasing." Paul picked up his own twig. "He got singled out. I don't know why, he was just a normal kid. But somehow, he got picked to be teased. It started with his name, and then it got worse. Pinecones in his sleeping bag, ants in his clothes. Laughing if he fumbled a ball. Calling him a wimp if he showed his feelings were hurt. Probably lots of other stuff I never knew about. He must have been miserable."

"Didn't he have any friends?" Rachel asked.

"Not any who really stood up for him," Paul said. "I told some kids to lay off a couple of times and so did one or two other guys. But I wasn't in Johnny's cabin, or his group. I always wished I'd done more for him, and now — " he stopped abruptly.

"Well, you were a kid, too," Rachel said. "And you didn't tease him, at least." She paused, started to ask a question. Then she realized she didn't really have to ask. "Mark and Steve — they did some of the teasing, I bet."

"They were the worst," Paul said. "Jordan was part of it, but he never started it. He just went along. Stacey got into it, too." He started snapping the twig into small pieces, shaking his head. "Poor kid. He wound up in the same cabin with Mark, Steve, and Jordan. Those three just wouldn't let up on him."

Rachel thought of the boy looking out at the lake. Johnny. Now she had a name for him. Maybe she hadn't imagined the sadness in that picture. "What happened to him?" she asked. "How did he die?"

It was on the wilderness hike, Paul told her. Johnny had left his tent during the night. Nobody knew why. Nobody even heard him. It was a bad night, lots of rain and wind. Some of the campers — Paul was one of them — found Johnny in the morning. They didn't even know he was gone yet. They were looking for dry firewood.

But they found Johnny.

"He must have gotten lost or something. And scared. He must have started running." Paul was sitting up straight now, like Rachel, his legs drawn up and his hands clasped tightly around them. "We found him down in this deep gully, lying next to an old tree trunk. They think he was running and he fell. His neck was broken."

Rachel's eyes stung with tears. The poor boy. To be teased into misery and then to die alone on a rainy night in the woods.

"I always wondered — " Paul broke off and got to his feet.

Rachel looked up at him. "You always wondered what?"

"Nothing. I just wondered why he left the tent that night," Paul said.

That wasn't what he'd been about to say, Rachel was sure. But she didn't call him on it. He obviously still felt bad about the boy. It wasn't fair to make him talk anymore if he didn't want to.

Paul held out his hand. Rachel took it and got to her feet. Still holding hands, they started back to the lakeshore.

The little beach was empty when they got back. Rachel and Paul started picking up the picnic things, polishing off the last of a bag of cookies while they did it. Before they were finished, people started appearing. Linda and Mark came out of the woods from one direction, Terry and Jordan from another. Steve was the last to show up, tossing rocks into the water as he ambled along the shoreline.

"What happened to everybody?" Linda asked as they all gathered together. "I must have walked miles and I couldn't find anyone."

"I got a little turned around," Jordan said.

"If I hadn't run into Terry, I'd probably still be wandering in the woods somewhere."

"You should have stuck with me," Steve told them. "You should see yourselves." He pulled a piece of bark out of Mark's hair. "You look like you've been logging."

"We were blazing trails, remember?" Mark said. "How come you're so neat and clean?"

"Because I stuck to the shoreline," Steve said. "Nice and cool. And no wildlife, if you know what I mean."

So Steve was finally able to joke about the snake, Rachel thought. It was good, except she wondered what he'd do when he saw that circle around his face. But maybe he wouldn't. Or maybe she'd take *that* picture down.

Everyone but Steve had twigs and bark and pine needles all over them, and all of them were hot. They went into the lake for another swim before heading back to camp, and that's when they noticed that Stacey was gone.

Rachel was floating on her back when Jordan surfaced beside her. He sluiced the water off his hair and looked around. "Hey, Rachel. Have you seen Stacey?"

Bringing her legs down, Rachel treaded water and looked toward the shore. Stacey wasn't there. "Maybe she decided to go into the woods after all."

"Yeah, that's probably it," Jordan said. He spun in the water and caught sight of Mark. "Hey, Mark! Did you see Stacey when you were coming back?"

Mark shook his head and dived under.

"Oh, well." Jordan chuckled. "She's probably wandering around cursing because she can't find us. Wait'll she comes back and sees we're all here — she'll really chew us out."

Rachel could picture it — Stacey emerging from the woods, hot and itchy and mad at everybody. She looked toward the shore again, half-expecting to see Stacey's blonde head appear. Steve, Terry, and Linda were sitting on the beach. Paul was wading in the shallow water and talking to them. Stacey wasn't there.

Next to Rachel, Jordan filled his lungs and dived under. In a moment, he surfaced next to Mark and the two of them started swimming slowly toward the shore. When the reached the others, Rachel saw them all talking and pointing toward the woods. Then they started putting on their shorts and shoes. Paul looked out at Rachel, cupped his hands, and shouted, "We're going to look for Stacey!"

Rachel waved to show she understood and watched them file off into the trees.

Rachel's legs were getting tired. She tried

to touch bottom, but she was too far out. The lake bed didn't go down gradually. About fifteen feet from the shore, there was a sudden, steep drop-off, and Rachel realized she was way past it. She lay back and floated again, feeling the warm sun on her eyelids.

Moving her hands and feet just enough to keep afloat, Rachel found herself thinking about Johnny Danard. And about the ones who'd teased him — Mark and Steve, Jordan and Stacey. She wondered if they felt guilty when he died, guilty for having made fun of him. At least one of them must have, because she figured it was one of them who took his picture down.

Unless Paul did it. He was the one who seemed to feel the worst about what had happened to Johnny. He didn't say he'd taken the picture, but he might not want her to know for some reason. Maybe she'd ask him.

She'd ask him about Steve's picture again, too. They hadn't finished talking about that, and she wanted to know what he thought about it all. Had somebody really put the snake in his sleeping bag? Or did someone just circle his face after it happened as a kind of sick joke?

That kind of joke was Mark's specialty, Rachel suddenly realized. Jordan's and Steve's and Stacey's, too, according to Paul. At least it used to be, and from everything Rachel had seen, they hadn't changed that much.

Of course, Steve wouldn't have drawn a circle around his own face. But one of the others might have. It was kind of a rotten thing to do, but it was better than thinking they'd deliberately put a snake in his bag. They'd probably done it just to be funny, just to single Steve out.

The way they'd singled out Johnny Danard.

The lake water lapped over Rachel's face suddenly, and she straightened up, treading again. Floating in a lake was a lot more work than floating in the ocean.

She was just about to head back to the shore when a movement farther out in the water caught her eye.

It was one of the rowboats, the old one, made out of wood.

Looking quickly at the shore, Rachel saw that the three boats they'd dragged up were still there. The other two had been tied up out of sight. Tim and Michelle had taken one of them. This one must have come loose somehow, and now it was floating farther and farther out.

But it wasn't floating very well, Rachel noticed. The front of it was tipped down, and the whole thing listed to one side. It must have been ripped when they dragged it over those jagged rocks, and now it was taking in water. She'd have to swim out and try to tow it in or it would sink.

Rachel took a breath and was just about to kick off when she saw that the boat wasn't empty.

Stacey was in it.

In a flash, Rachel realized what must have happened. Stacey had taken Paul's advice and gone to lie down in the boat, where it was shady. She'd fallen asleep, and then the boat had come loose somehow. It hadn't been very far out of the water anyway, and once it was free, it had just drifted away.

Stacey hadn't seen Rachel yet. In fact, she looked like she'd just woken up and discovered her situation. Half of her hair was soaking wet. The water had probably sloshed in and jolted her awake. She wasn't wearing the life jacket she'd worn on the way over.

Even though Rachel was too far away to see her expression, she knew Stacey must be ready to panic.

"Stacey!" Rachel hollered. "Hang on! I'll come get you!"

Gripping the side of the boat with one hand, Stacey shaded her eyes with the other and looked across the water. When she saw Rachel, she tried to stand up.

"Sit down!" Rachel shouted. She started swimming, hoping Stacey had enough sense to just hold on to the boat. She swam for a short distance.

But when she heard Stacey screaming, she stopped for a second.

The front of the boat was tipped even farther down now. Stacey was sitting again, and Rachel couldn't understand why she didn't move to the back.

Stacey screamed again. And again.

She looked like she was trying to move, but she wasn't going anywhere. Her movements were jerky — she looked like she was tugging at something.

Finally her words carried clearly across the water.

"My foot! Rachel, I can't get my foot out!"

Then Rachel understood. When Stacey stood up, she must have stepped right on the weakened part where the water was coming in. Her weight had driven her foot through the wood, and now she couldn't get it loose.

She was trapped in the sinking boat.

Chapter 16

Rachel's tiredness disappeared, and now she felt a strong jolt of energy. Plunging forward, she started pulling herself through the water with smooth, steady strokes. Her thoughts raced along with her body.

She had to hurry.

Stacey was probably hysterical by now. The harder she struggled to free herself, the faster the boat would go down.

As Rachel raced through the water, she could hear Stacey screaming the way she had before, when Steve threw her in.

Sharp, high-pitched screams, full of fear.

Just like Steve and the snake, this was the worst thing that could happen to Stacey. Rachel didn't know if the boat would actually pull Stacey down with it. She had no idea how long the boat would float. She just knew Stacey wouldn't be able to handle this.

Stacey needed help or else she'd drown in the lake that terrified her so much.

Rachel pulled up for a second to get her bearings. She was only about twenty feet from the boat. Its front was completely under water now. Stacey's voice was getting ragged and hoarse from the piercing screams.

Rachel gasped in some air and plunged ahead.

Stroking forward, Rachel's left arm smacked into the boat. She got a good hold of it and was pushing the hair out of her eyes so she could see.

Suddenly Stacey's hand clamped down on her wrist.

"Get me out of here!" Stacey shrieked. "I'm going to die if you don't get me out of here!"

"I will!" Rachel gasped. "Let go of my hand. I need both hands. Stacey, let go!"

Stacey's blue eyes were wide, filled with terror. Her lips were clamped shut now, her teeth clenched.

"Stacey, let go!" Rachel yelled. "I can't help if you don't let go!"

Stacey tightened her grip. Her fingernails dug painfully into Rachel's skin. She was looking at Rachel, but she didn't seem to see her.

Rachel reached up with her other hand and tried to pry Stacey's fingers loose, kicking the whole time to keep herself afloat. She managed to get a good hold on Stacey's thumb, and without worrying about how much it might hurt, she bent it backward toward her wrist.

Stacey yelped and yanked her hand away. She looked at Rachel as if she'd like to kill her. Then she started to cry.

"Sorry," Rachel gasped. "Now don't grab me again."

Steadying herself on the side of the boat, Rachel lifted herself up a little and looked in. Stacey's foot had broken through one of the bottom boards up to her ankle. Splintered wood dug into her bare leg; Rachel could see where Stacey'd cut herself trying to pull her foot loose.

"Okay," she said her voice breathless but firm. "Stacey. I'm going under the boat and see if I can yank the board down some more. Then you can pull your foot back out. Don't worry. Everything's going to be all right. Okay, Stacey?"

Stacey was still crying and didn't answer.

Rachel pushed back from the boat. Filling her lungs with air, she flipped headfirst under the water. She didn't have to dive far, but even so, she could feel the water pressing down on her and the blood pounding in her head.

It was dark under the water, and Rachel had to feel her way. Trailing one hand along the boat's underside, using the other to pull herself with, she made her way underneath the boat.

Something sharp and jagged scraped against her hand. She almost jerked away before she realized it was the broken wood. She felt with her other hand, touched skin, and knew it was Stacey's foot. She felt a splinter slicing into her hand as she grabbed the wood and pulled.

If she'd been standing on the ground, it would have been easy. But floundering under water, Rachel couldn't get any strength into her pull.

Her head was pounding now and her lungs felt ready to burst. She was starting to panic herself. She knew she'd have to go up for air in seconds or she'd pass out.

Rachel gave the wood one final tug. She was sure it wasn't enough, but she had to let go. She had to breathe. She kicked away from the boat and thrashed through the water, desperate for air.

When she broke the surface, she dragged in great gulps of air, coughing and choking as the water lapped into her mouth. She could hear herself breathing hoarsely, and she couldn't seem to keep from swallowing water. She was exhausted. She wanted to lie back and float.

She knew she had to go back under.

"Hurry!" she heard Stacey shouting. "Hurry up, the boat's sinking!"

"I'm trying," Rachel said. It was almost a whisper. She couldn't get enough air to shout.

"Mark, hurry!" Stacey yelled. "Mark, Jordan!"

Then Stacey's face appeared over the side of the boat. "Rachel!" she said. "It's okay, you got the wood loose enough and I pulled my foot free. Mark and Jordan are rowing out here!" Her cheeks were stained with tear tracks. She wiped at them and her lips trembled. "Thanks, Rachel," she murmured.

"Yeah," Rachel sighed. She was too tired to say anything else. She pushed wet strands of hair out of her eyes and breathed deeply. Then she lay on her back and floated until the other boat reached them.

Paul and Linda rigged up a line to tow the broken boat back to camp. They were still out on the water when Rachel and the others reached the dock. Tim and Michelle were full of questions, but Rachel was too tired to say much. All she wanted was a shower and a nap.

Stumbling up the path, she almost bumped into Mr. Drummond.

"What happened?" he asked, looking toward the dock where the others were still gathered.

"An accident," Rachel said. "One of the boats almost sank."

He shifted his gaze to her face. "And was anyone hurt?"

He looked grim, Rachel thought, as if he expected the worst. "Not really," she said. "Just some splinters. Everyone's okay."

The groundskeeper's eyes narrowed, and he slowly shook his head. Then he turned and walked toward the lodge.

Rachel shivered, but she didn't know if it was because of Mr. Drummond, or because she was cold and exhausted.

Still shivering, she walked to the shower cabin and peeled off her swimsuit. The water was hot for the first time since she'd been there. It stung her hand where she'd pulled out a splinter, but she didn't care. She stood under the weak spray, waiting for the cold to seep out of her bones. When the hot water ran out, she dried off and put on her shorts and T-shirt. Then she walked up to the cabin and fell facedown on top of her sleeping bag.

She thought she'd be dead to the world, but she kept waking with a start, forgetting where she was. Then she'd drift off again. She was aware of the other girls coming in and out of the cabin. She heard them whispering for a while, and then they were quiet. Had they left?

Had everyone gone? Rachel wanted to open her eyes and see, but the lids were too heavy to lift. So was her head. She nestled it deeper into the pillow and finally fell into a deep sleep.

When she woke, the cabin was dark. Not the deep dark of the night, though. Just kind of a hazy, gray dark. Her stomach rumbled and she figured it was past dinnertime. She slid a leg off the bed, then another, and finally pushed herself to the floor. Picking up Stacey's clock, she saw that it was seven-thirty. Definitely time to eat.

Her clothes were rumpled and wrinkled, so she changed into a fresh shirt and jeans. She knew her hair must be mashed on one side. Yawning, she tugged her brush through it a few times. By then she was starving, so she left the cabin and headed down the path to the lodge. As she got closer, she could smell the food. Hamburgers. Her stomach growled again and she picked up her pace.

As soon as she opened the door, she heard Stacey. "I don't care! I think we should call the police!" Her voice wasn't as panicked as when she'd been on the lake, but it was close.

"Stacey, we really shouldn't jump to conclusions." That was Tim. His tone reminded Rachel of her dentist, calm and soothing. "Let's think about this first."

"I don't have to think!" Stacey said. "I know! I was the one out there on the lake, not you. And I'm not jumping to any conclusions!"

Wondering what was going on, Rachel walked into the main room. Everyone was sitting at the tables, and they turned to look at her when she came in.

"Rachel, hi," Terry said. "We went ahead and started eating. You were out like a light and we didn't want to wake you."

"That's okay." Rachel walked over and pulled out a chair at the empty place, next to Paul. "What's happening?" she asked. "Why are we calling the police?"

"We're not." Smiling, Tim stood up. "Listen, I've got to go talk to Michelle about that delivery of towels. It never came." He picked up his plate and started out. "Take it easy, everybody," he called over his shoulder.

When he was gone, Rachel asked again, "What's happening?"

Stacey started to answer, but Linda stopped her. "Wait. If Rachel's going to hear this, she needs food. Besides, she's the heroine, right?" She was already on her way to the kitchen. "Sit there, Rachel. I'll bring your dinner."

Rachel was still a little groggy and she didn't feel like playing a guessing game. "Will somebody just tell me what's going on?"

"A mystery's afloat. No, afoot," Mark said. He was trying to be funny, but he looked serious. No, not serious. Worried.

Steve looked worried, too. They all looked worried, now that Rachel thought about it. She glanced at Paul and raised her eyebrows, questioning. He shook his head.

What did that mean?

That there was nothing to be worried about?

Linda was coming back now, a plate in her hands. She put it in front of Rachel and then sat down. Rachel forked up a bite of salad, swallowed, and said, "Okay. Tell me."

"Somebody's out to get us," Stacey said immediately. "First Steve, then me."

"And who will be the next lucky victim?" Mark said in a ghoulish voice.

"It's not funny!" Stacey said.

"Come on, you guys." Rachel thumped some ketchup onto her hamburger. "You're not making any sense, and you're starting to scare me."

"We should be scared," Stacey said. She shoved her plate away and leaned forward, her elbows on the table. "The boat, Rachel. It was tied up when I got into it. It didn't untie itself, right?"

Rachel frowned. She hadn't thought about it at the time. She'd just gone to help Stacey, and then she'd gone to sleep.

But Stacey was right. The boat hadn't untied itself.

"It's the only wooden boat left," Stacey went on. "It probably got ripped up when we pulled it out of the water, because I would have woken up if someone had started ripping at it. But somebody untied it, that's for sure. All it took was an easy little shove, and I was gone."

Rachel's stomach tightened. She suddenly wasn't that hungry anymore. "You really think someone did that? Knowing you were in it?"

Stacey nodded.

Mark cleared his throat. "There was last night, too. The snake, remember?"

"You're asking me?" Steve said. He laughed nervously. "I'll forget it in a couple of decades or so. Maybe."

"Stacey thinks it's Mr. Drummond," Linda said.

Rachel stared. "Mr. Drummond was over here today. How could he have done anything to the boat?"

"Rachel, there are other ways to get across the lake besides going *on* the lake," Stacey said. "The guy's a creep, I already told you that."

"He wouldn't do it," Paul said.

Linda frowned at him. "How do you know?"

Paul sighed and shook his head. "I guess I

don't know for sure. I just don't believe he's the monster Stacey thinks he is."

"Well, if it's not him, then it's somebody else," Stacey insisted. "These things aren't happening by themselves. Somebody's doing it." She shoved her chair back and stood up. "We're not that far from civilization, you know. There are little towns around. Maybe there's even a prison."

"Why would an escaped prisoner bother with us?" Paul asked.

"Who knows?" Stacey was pacing back and forth, her arms wrapped around herself. "But somebody is. Somebody's out to get us. A prisoner, a killer, I don't know! A maniac!"

Her voice rose on the word "maniac," and everyone was quiet for a moment. Rachel felt a kind of chill settle over the room.

"It's very strange," Terry said thoughtfully. "*If* someone is doing these things, then they've picked what scares us the most."

"What do you mean, Terry?" Linda asked quietly.

"I mean Steve's scared of snakes, and Stacey's scared of the lake," Terry explained. "It's just weird, that's all. Isn't it?"

The others started talking again, but Rachel sat silent, thinking about what Terry had said. If she was right, if somebody was using the things that scared people the most, then it wasn't an escaped prisoner. It wasn't a maniac on the loose. It was somebody who knew all of them.

And the only people who knew were right here at Camp Silverlake.

Rachel clasped her hands together to keep them steady. She looked down at her plate and saw that the grease had congealed under her hamburger. She hadn't even taken a bite and now she definitely wasn't hungry.

Everyone here knew, she thought. Linda and Terry. Mark and Jordan. And Paul. If any of them wanted to terrorize Steve and Stacey, they all knew exactly how to do it. And they'd had the time, too. They'd been separated last night, and they'd all gone off in different directions today.

She already wondered whether someone had put the snake in Steve's bag. And now Stacey and the boat. They weren't just two horrible coincidences.

Suddenly, Rachel remembered. Everyone was still talking, going over and over the possibilities. Slowly, trying to look casual, Rachel got up. She took her plate with her, to make them think she was going to the kitchen. In the entryway, she stopped in front of the bulletin board.

The light was dim, but Rachel didn't need a spotlight to see.

Two circles had been drawn around Stacey's face.

Last night, Steve had been the target. Today it was Stacey.

Who would be next?

Chapter 17

Everyone's jumping at shadows now, thinking there's a killer on the loose. A psycho, a maniac. What a strange feeling to hear those words. To hear them and know I'm the one they're talking about.

I got lucky with the boat. I didn't even know it was damaged. I wanted to do it myself, but it would have been too risky. Then nature stepped in and made my plan work even better.

They don't know, of course. They have no idea. It was hard to hear them make their wild guesses, to pretend I had nothing to do with it.

But I have to wait. It's not finished yet. Soon, though, I'm almost there.

Rachel was in the water again. She was swimming toward the boat, but it kept moving away. Every time she stopped to catch her breath and look, the boat was just as far away as it was when she'd started. She couldn't give up, though. She had to keep going. Stacey was in the boat, and if Rachel didn't help her, she'd die. So she kept on swimming, even though she was getting tired. She didn't think she'd make it, but she did. She bumped her hand on the side of the boat and then she grabbed hold of it. She'd made it.

"I'm here," she said. "Where are you?"

Somebody loked over the side of the boat. But it wasn't Stacey. It was a boy with shaggy brown hair and a sad look in his eyes. "You're too late," he said to Rachel.

"No, I'm here," Rachel said.

The boy shook his head. "You're too late," he said again. "I'm already dead."

"Johnny!" Rachel cried. "Johnny!"

Rachel woke from the dream and sat straight up, her heart pounding, her breath coming in gulps. The cabin was dark. She could hear someone moving around, but she couldn't see who it was. She pushed herself back in the bed, not sure whether to scream or keep quiet.

The the light came on, blinding her, and she heard Terry's voice. "Rachel. Rachel, are you okay?"

Squinting in the glare, Rachel nodded. "I had a dream. Did I yell or something?"

"Loud enough to wake me up," Stacey said.

"Me too." Linda sat up and pushed back her coppery, tangled hair. "What was it all about, Rachel?"

Rachel shook her head. "Just a dream. It didn't make much sense."

"You called out somebody's name." Linda sat crosslegged on her bed and smiled. "A boy's name."

"Johnny," Terry said. "You called for Johnny."

"I know," Rachel said.

"So who is he?" Terry asked. "A boyfriend you never told us about?"

"No." Rachel glanced at Stacey, who was looking at her curiously. She hadn't wanted to talk about Johnny Danard in front of Stacey, but maybe it didn't matter. Maybe Stacey didn't have any horrible memories about it. "I was dreaming about a boy who was at camp here one summer," she said. "His name was Johnny Danard."

Stacey flinched at the name, as if she'd been hit. Then she sat forward, her face hard and angry. "What are you trying to do, Rachel? Is this a sick joke or something?"

"Stacey! What's the matter?" Terry asked. "Who is this boy?"

"He was just a kid who went to camp here one summer," Stacey said impatiently. "And he died, okay? He had an accident and he died, but it was a long time ago." She looked at Rachel. "How did you know about him? Who told you?"

"Paul," Rachel said. "Paul told me after I put his picture up. Remember the picture of that boy I put in the middle of the bulletin board?" She suddenly wondered if Stacey had taken the picture. But she didn't ask. "It's not there anymore, but that was Johnny."

"Yeah, you told me about that," Linda said. She was staring into the distance, as if she were looking at the photograph. "He was standing on the dock, wasn't he?"

"I'm not sure I even noticed it," Terry said. "But anyway, what happened to him?"

Rachel decided not to tell the details. "Just what Stacey said. He died in an accident." She rushed on, wanting to get off the subject of his death. "I was dreaming about Stacey and the boat, but he got mixed up in it. You know how crazy dreams are. Sorry I woke everybody up."

"Did Paul ever tell you what happened?" Linda asked. "What kind of accident it was?"

"He fell," Rachel said. "I guess no one was ever really sure how it happened, though."

"How awful," Terry said with a shudder. "Stacey, you were here. Did you know him? Did you see him?"

"No!" Stacey cried. "I didn't see him and I hardly knew him. You'll have to talk to somebody else if you want all the gory details. Isn't there enough going on without worrying about some kid who died way in the past? Could we just please drop it?"

Terry looked at her thoughtfully. "Sure. Okay, Stacey. If it bothers you that much, we'll drop it."

"Good!" Stacey blew out a breath and stood up. "Maybe we can go back to sleep now. Is that all right with you, Rachel?"

Without waiting for Rachel to answer, Stacey reached up and yanked on the light string. The last thing Rachel saw before the cabin went dark were Stacey's blue eyes, glaring down at her.

Everyone was quiet at breakfast the next morning. Tim and Michelle ate with them, and it was obvious they didn't want to hear any wild rumors about escaped prisoners or maniacs stalking Camp Silverlake. They kept up a steady stream of conversation about chores and projects and what to do if a camper got hurt or homesick.

No one had fixed scrambled eggs this morning, but no one seemed very hungry anyway. Well, Rachel was. In spite of feeling troubled and edgy, her stomach was empty from last night. She ate two bowls of cereal, but she didn't really taste it.

She hadn't dreamed again, of Johnny Danard or anyone else. But when she woke up, she felt like she'd been battling demons all night.

It was partly Stacey, of course. She'd never expected anything like Stacey's reaction. All it took was Johnny's name, and Stacey was on the defensive, yelling and practically accusing Rachel of . . . of what, though? Of trying to make her feel guilty and ashamed? That must be it. Stacey felt guilty for teasing the poor kid, and she thought Rachel was going to rub it in. Rachel wanted to talk to her, tell her it wasn't true. All during breakfast she tried to catch Stacey's eye. But Stacey sat with Jordan, and never looked in Rachel's direction.

Stacey wasn't the only problem, though. Rachel didn't believe in the maniac theory, but what she *did* believe was almost as bad — that someone here at camp was playing dangerous games. The snake and the boat weren't coincidences. She had the circles on the picture to prove it.

She didn't think anyone else had noticed the

circles because no one had said anything. She'd decided to take the picture down after breakfast, but she didn't get a chance. Tim and Michelle were determined to keep everyone busy, probably so they wouldn't have a chance to come up with any more scary rumors. As soon as the last bite of cereal was gone, they hustled everyone outside and sent them off to clean the shower cabins and touch up the paint on some of the sleeping cabins.

"Rachel?" Paul caught up to her as she was walking along a path carrying a mop and a bucket full of cleaning supplies. "Hey, I wish we had telephones in the cabins," he said. "I would have called you last night."

"That would have been nice," she said. "What would you have said?"

"I'd have asked if you'd seen the circles around Stacey's face."

Rachel stopped walking. "Yes. I saw them. I take it you did, too."

He nodded.

"It's scary," Rachel said. She looked around and saw Stacey walking with Jordan. Linda was heading up another path, swinging a bucket of paint in her hand. Rachel looked back at Paul and shivered. "I dreamed about Johnny Danard last night," she said. "I called his name in my sleep, and I woke everybody up. So naturally, they wanted to know who Johnny was. When I told them, Stacey almost freaked out. Like she thought I talked about him on purpose, to make her feel bad."

"Rachel." Paul stepped closer and put his hand around her arm. "Be careful."

"Don't worry, I will be." She laughed a little. "But my picture's not on the bulletin board, remember? Nobody can draw circles around my face. I'm safe." She was trying to joke, but the situation wasn't very funny. "I want to tell everybody about it, about the circles, but I don't know who to tell."

"You mean because one of us is doing it." Paul's hand tightened on her arm. "Just be careful, Rachel."

Paul's voice sounded strange, Rachel thought. As if he wasn't just concerned about her but was . . . *warning* her.

What had he said? *"One of us is doing it."*

What if *he* was the one?

Rachel stepped back a little, trying to smile. "Sure. I'll be careful," she said. "Listen, I should get to work. I'll talk to you later."

He couldn't be the one, Rachel thought as she walked away. She liked him too much. Oh, sure, that was a great reason.

No, but he couldn't be. Why would he do anything to Steve and Stacey? She didn't think he liked them much, but that was no reason to sabotage a boat and put a rattlesnake in a sleeping bag.

Then she remembered Johnny Danard. Paul knew what they'd done to him. He'd seen them play tricks on him and make his life miserable. Was he trying to pay them back somehow, for Johnny? Pay them back with some tricks of his own?

Rachel kept shaking her head, trying to shake these thoughts away. If Paul was the one, he wouldn't have warned *her*, because she didn't have anything to do with Johnny. She'd never been at Camp Silverlake before. Anyway, there was probably no connection between the snake and the boat and the boy who'd died seven years ago. That's why Paul had warned her. Of course it was. Everybody could be a target. Even Paul.

Even Rachel.

Chapter 18

Cleaning the shower cabin should have taken about an hour, but Rachel managed to stretch it to two. It gave her the same feeling washing dishes did — she could concentrate completely on scrubbing and mopping and rinsing. She didn't have to think about anything if she didn't want to. And she didn't want to, so she took her time.

She raised blisters on two fingers scrubbing out every corner of every shower stall. She mopped the floor three times. When she was done, her eyes were watering from the smell of the fake pine cleaner. If the place weren't made mostly of cement, it would have sparkled.

Stepping outside, Rachel tossed out the bucket of dirty water and took a breath of fresh air. The wind was blowing again high up in the trees. She loved the sound. She wished it could blow away all the thoughts that came rushing back the minute she stopped her manual labor.

Stacey. Maybe she'd try to find Stacey and talk to her. They were going to be working together for five weeks, after all. It wasn't going to be much fun if Stacey held a grudge against her all that time.

Setting the bucket and mop down, Rachel started along the path toward the rainy-day building. Stacey was checking all the arts and crafts supplies so she could tell Tim what to order. At least, that's what Rachel had heard her say earlier.

Rachel found Jordan in the building alone, idly shoving a Nok-Hockey puck back and forth along the board. "Hi, Jordan." She leaned against the door frame and smiled. "That's kind of hard to play alone, isn't it?"

"Yeah." Jordan hardly glanced at her. He kept shoving the puck with one hand, catching it with the other, and shooting it back. "I'm not playing a game, though. What about you?"

"Me? What are you talking about?"

Jordan shrugged, his eyes on the board. "Never mind."

"Well, okay." Rachel decided he was in one of his moods. She was glad she hadn't gone for a walk with him that night, to "get to know him better." She didn't want to know him better. "Listen, I'm looking for Stacey," she said.

"I thought she'd be in here. Do you know where she went?"

Still not looking at her, Jordan shrugged again.

Rachel felt her temper rise. "What does that mean?" she asked. "Do you know or don't you?"

"No. I don't know where Stacey went." He slammed the puck down. "Okay?"

"What's your problem, Jordan?" Rachel asked hotly. "If you're going to be mad, you could at least tell me the reason."

"I'm not mad, I'm just — " Jordan took a breath and looked at her. He gave her a smile, not a big one, but big enough for his dimple to show. "Nothing. Sorry."

Rachel was mad herself now, and his cute smile didn't make any difference. She turned around and left.

She didn't care what was bothering Jordan. She didn't care where Stacey was anymore, either. She'd been by herself for two hours, but she wouldn't mind being alone all day if it would keep her from having to put up with people's moods. Besides, the shower cabin might be spotless, but her clothes were pretty grubby. She'd go to the cabin and change. Write a letter to her parents. Try to forget what was going on, for just a little while, anyway.

The cabin was empty and cool. The shades

were still down and it was dim inside. Rachel went to her bed, pulling off her T-shirt as she walked. The shirt's neck was a little tight. She was tugging it up over her face, not able to see anything, when she bumped into her cot. She reached down to the bed to catch herself. Her hands landed on something soft. Dry. Thick and round, like a piece of rope. But it wasn't rope.

Rachel knew what it was, and she felt her stomach turn.

She whipped the shirt off and looked down.

It was the dead rattlesnake.

The two pieces of its body had been coiled on top of her sleeping bag. The ends where it had been cut were crusty with congealed blood.

In the middle of the coil, buried almost to the handle in the folds of the sleeping bag, was a butcher knife.

Chapter 19

Rachel had known it was the snake. She'd been expecting the snake.

But not the knife.

Her stomach had been churning before she'd even got the shirt off. Now, seeing the knife, she felt a sour taste rise in her throat and she was sure she was going to throw up.

Spinning away from the bed, she ran to the cabin door and leaned out, taking in big gulps of air, swallowing hard. After a minute or two, her stomach settled down and she knew she wouldn't be sick.

She stayed where she was a moment, still breathing deeply. Then she went back into the cabin. Deliberately not looking at the hideous thing on her bed, she pulled out her duffle bag. She took out clean shorts and a shirt and put them on, stuffing the dirty clothes into her laundry bag. Then she combed her fingers through her hair. Finally, she looked at her bed again.

Okay. It was horrible and scary, but it was dead. Before she thought about who and why, she'd get rid of it. She turned away again, looking for something to put it in, a sack or a garbage bag. She saw a paper sack sticking out from under Terry's cot and she was on her knees, sliding it out, when Terry's voice made her jump.

"What are you doing?" Terry sounded almost angry.

Rachel slid the sack all the way out and held it up. "I needed a bag, Terry. I saw this one under your bed, that's all."

Terry stepped farther into the cabin, her eyes searching Rachel's face. "Couldn't you have asked?"

"You weren't here. You act like I was going through your things or something." Rachel stood up and put the sack on Terry's bed. "If you don't want me to use it, I won't, okay?"

"No, I'm sorry. Go ahead, take it," Terry said. "Sorry. I guess I'm a little jumpy with everything that's been going on."

"You and me both." Rachel nodded at her own bed. "Somebody left me a present."

Terry looked across at Rachel's bed and gasped. "God!" She stepped closer and peered down at the snake and the knife. "Rachel, this is really terrible!"

"It almost made me sick," Rachel said.

"No wonder." Terry straightened up and looked at Rachel. "It's happened again. To you, this time."

Rachel shuddered.

"I've got to get out of here," Terry said. "Sorry, Rachel. I just can't stand to look at it." She hurried across the cabin and out the door.

Well, thanks a lot, Rachel thought. The snake was on *her* bed, not Terry's. She was the one who ought to be running away.

Angry and upset, Rachel snapped open the paper sack and gingerly dropped the pieces of dead snake into it. Then she pulled out the knife and turned it over in her hands. The blade gleamed in the dim light.

Mr. Drummond had killed the snake. He'd chopped it in half and carried it away on the shovel. Rachel thought he'd buried it. What had he done with it?

Carrying the knife and the sack, Rachel left the cabin and went to look for the grounds-keeper. She found him in the storage cabin, sorting through some of the tools. "Mr. Drummond."

He looked at her, standing in the doorway.

Rachel held up the sack. "I found this just a little while ago," she said. "It's the snake you killed."

His face tightened. "The trash can lids — animals can't get them open."

So he'd put it in a trash can, Rachel thought. And someone took it out. Was it Mr. Drummond? He hadn't asked her where she found it. Wasn't he curious, or did he already know?

"Well," she said. "It got out somehow. I'd like to bury it. Could I borrow a shovel?"

Mr. Drummond shook his head and held out his hand. "Give it to me. I'll take care of it."

Like the last time? Rachel thought. "Thanks, but I don't mind doing it," she said. "I'm sure you've got other stuff to do."

He nodded, his bald head shiny in the light. Then he turned away to pick out a shovel. The shovels and rakes were hanging on the back wall. Next to them was a rifle, its barrel pointing to the floor. Rachel swallowed and suddenly wished she hadn't come here.

Mr. Drummond was coming back, a shovel in his hand. When he gave it to her, he noticed the knife she was holding.

"Is this yours?" she asked.

"No. It's a kitchen knife."

"That's what I thought," she told him. "I'll put it back."

"Where did you find it?"

"Oh . . . around." Rachel was ready to leave. If he'd put the snake on her bed, he obviously wasn't going to admit it. Besides, he made her nervous. So did the gun. "Well, thanks, Mr. Drummond," she said. "I'll bring the shovel back in a little while."

"The snake," he said.

"Yes?"

The groundskeeper's lips curved in a tiny smile. "Bury it deep."

Rachel did bury it deep. Way beyond the cabins, she found a tiny clearing in the woods where the ground was soft enough to dig, and she buried the snake at least three feet down. She pounded the dirt down with the shovel, then kicked pine needles over it all. She was certain no one saw her. If the snake was taken out again, an animal would have to do it.

But this time not a human animal, she thought grimly.

Lunch was not a cheerful gathering. Stacey was still grumpy, and she huddled with Mark and Steve, talking softly. Jordan sat with them, but he looked miserable and didn't join in the conversation.

Rachel kept seeing the dead snake on her

bed and then she'd blink the ugly image away. Paul looked at her, his eyes questioning, but Rachel didn't feel like talking about it yet.

After Tim and Michelle left, Terry quietly asked if Rachel was okay. But not quietly enough.

Rachel felt everyone's eyes on her.

"What happened?" Linda asked.

"It was the snake," Terry said. "It was sitting on Rachel's bed. And there was a knife, too. It was hideous."

Everyone was quiet for a moment. Paul reached over and squeezed Rachel's hand. "You're okay?" he murmured.

"Yes. Fine." Rachel drank some water.

"Well, it looks like you've joined the club with me and Steve," Stacey said. "How does it feel?"

Rachel didn't answer. Although she wasn't sure why, something about the dead snake seemed different from the other two incidents.

"How do you think it feels?" Terry asked Stacey angrily. "You should have seen her face when I walked in."

Terry didn't mention that she hadn't stuck around to help out, Rachel noticed.

"What did you do with the snake, Rachel?" Mark's eerie blue eyes sparkled with curiosity. "Are you going to keep it as a souvenir?"

"That's an awful thing to say," Terry said. She kept licking her lips nervously.

"I got rid of it," Rachel told Mark. "I don't think anybody can find it now."

"It was just a dead snake," Steve said. "A live one, now that's different."

"It wasn't just a dead snake," Terry argued. "It was like a . . . like a warning."

A warning. Rachel's hand shook a little as she put her water glass down. Paul had warned her, just a few hours ago. Be careful, he'd said. Did he know something was about to happen? Did he do it himself?

The snake and the knife. Terry was right — it was like a warning. Did that mean there was something worse yet to come?

"Rachel, are you sure you're okay?" Linda's voice broke into her thoughts.

"Sure," Rachel said.

"You looked so worried." Linda leaned on the table, her amber eyes full of sympathy. "If you want to stay here at camp this afternoon, everybody'll understand."

"Stay here at camp?" Rachel gave her head a little shake. "I must have missed something. Where are you going?"

"Hiking," Steve said. "We'll check out another trail and leave Camp Silverlake and all our fears behind."

"No, I'll come," Rachel said. "It'll feel good to get away."

"Are you sure, Rachel?" Stacey asked. "After all, we will have to come back."

"What does that mean?" Linda asked.

"You never know what might be waiting for us when we come back, that's all." Stacey looked away.

But Rachel had seen the glint in those eyes. Was that why Stacey didn't seem very sympathetic about the dead snake on Rachel's bed? Because she knew who put it there?

Because *she'd* done it herself?

Rachel saw Jordan and Stacey exchange glances. Had they both been in on it?

Jordan. Still quiet, not meeting her eye. He'd been so cold before when she'd asked him where Stacey was. Accusing her of playing a game. And then he'd smiled at her. It was just like Jordan — to be in on the plot, to go along with it. But to try to stay on her good side with that smile.

What game did they think she could possibly be playing with them, though? Did they think she was behind the other two incidents? That she was the "psycho" terrorizing the camp?

Last night, when Rachel had her nightmare and then talked about Johnny, Stacey had practically accused her of being up to something.

"What do you know about it?" she'd asked. *"What are you trying to do?"*

Was that it? Rachel wondered. She knew they'd teased the boy and played tricks on him. They didn't want her to talk about it. She'd seen them together this morning, she remembered, talking quietly, heads together. Was that when they came up with their "warning"?

It made some sense. But not much. Paul knew all about what they'd done to Johnny, too. He was the one who'd told her, but they hadn't done anything to him. Maybe he'd be next. Maybe she should tell Paul to be careful.

But Rachel couldn't quite believe it. They'd been mean to someone and they were ashamed of it. Okay. She understood that. But to play such a sick joke on her just because of that was crazy.

If they did it, they weren't just telling her to be quiet. They were warning her about something else. There was something else they wanted to hide.

Chapter 20

*The snake. What a great trick, bringing it back
again. The knife was a clever touch, too. If I
didn't know better, I'd say some maniac was
on the loose!*

*I shouldn't joke about it. But it's hard some-
times, to see them all so scared and confused,
and keep a straight face. I have to look away,
or get away, just so they won't know. Then
when I'm alone, I can smile.*

*I don't smile for long, of course. Because
nothing is truly funny anymore. And when I'm
with them, my smiles are false. So is my fear.
That's hard, too, pretending all the time.*

*Well. Time to go. Time to pretend. It's hard,
but it's getting easier. I can almost see the end
now.*

"Terry, aren't you coming?" Rachel asked.
She and Linda were heading out of the cabin,

where they'd changed into jeans for the hike. Terry was still inside, sitting on her bed. "Everybody else is waiting up at the lodge."

"Okay." Terry stood up, a troubled look on her face. "I don't really want to go. But I don't want to stay here alone, either." She sighed and joined the other two outside.

"So who do you think left the snake on your bed?" Linda asked Rachel.

"Maybe a ghost left it," Terry said suddenly.

Rachel and Linda stopped walking and stared at her.

Terry laughed a little. "I know, it sounds crazy. But Rachel, I was thinking about that boy you told us about. Johnny." She hunched her shoulders and looked around. "He died, you said. Maybe his spirit is haunting this place, seeking revenge."

"Why would it be seeking revenge?" Rachel asked.

"Maybe revenge is the wrong word," Terry said. "But a happy spirit wouldn't put a snake in Steve's sleeping bag or try to drown Stacey."

"I can't believe we're talking about ghosts," Linda said. "Everybody knows there aren't any ghosts. It's ridiculous."

"Okay, forget it," Terry said quietly. "I shouldn't have said anything. I know it was crazy."

Linda smiled at her. "Let's get out of here, okay? I bet when we're away from this place, we'll all relax."

Rachel hoped so. Walking toward the lodge, she thought about what Terry said. A ghost. An unhappy spirit. In a way, it was true. Whoever was doing these things must be very unhappy.

But it wasn't a ghost.

Whoever was doing it was also very much alive.

They took a different trail this time, not the one that would lead them to the lookout. Mark seemed relieved, Rachel noticed. Maybe he remembered the trail and knew that there weren't any steep drops along the way.

The trail needed a lot of clearing. The winter winds had ripped off hundreds of branches, and they littered the trail like giant, ragged toothpicks. Then came the spring growth, and dense vines had spread out, so thick they sometimes covered the trail completely.

No one had thought to wear gloves, and by the time they'd reached a clearing where they could rest, their hands and arms were blistered and stinging with scratches.

"I think I might sue," Steve said, as they all flopped down in the clearing. "When I got this job, no one said anything about backbreaking labor." He held out a hand and pointed to an enormous blister on the palm. "Look at this! I'm wounded!"

"You think that's bad?" Jordan held out his arm and pulled up his shirtsleeve, revealing a long scratch that was seeping blood. "*That's* a wound."

"Ha." Linda pulled off a sneaker and sock and stuck her left foot up in the air. "There's a blister on my heel, see it? Hands and arms don't count. You don't have to walk on your hands."

Terry laughed. "I have a big scratch on my nose. Does that count?"

"Only if you're so wounded you can't smell Linda's foot," Mark said.

Everyone laughed and kept on comparing blisters and scratches to see who'd suffered the most. It seemed like forever since they'd laughed together, Rachel thought. Even Stacey had dropped her attitude and was arguing with Paul, telling him broken fingernails were a much bigger problem than torn jeans. Clearing the trail was just like cleaning the shower cabin — they'd thrown themselves into the work and forgotten about everything else.

The laughter died down, but the good feeling seemed to hang on. They drank the juice they'd brought, and then struggled to their feet.

"Onward," Steve said, brandishing a stick in the air.

"Onward where?" Stacey asked. "I thought this was the end."

"You wish," Mark said. He pointed ahead, to what seemed like a wall of trees. "The trail leads thataway."

"Nope." Steve shook his head and pointed in another direction. "It's this way."

"Let's pretend this is the end and forget it," Stacey suggested.

"Who do you think's right, Jordan?" Linda asked.

Jordan looked in the directions Steve and Mark were pointing. Then he shrugged. "I give up." Decisive as always, Rachel thought.

"Paul?" Linda asked.

"Steve's right," Paul said. "I think."

Rachel and Terry and Linda had no idea, but everyone else except Mark thought Steve had it right.

"There's an easy way to settle this," Mark said. "I go my way, and the rest of you unbelievers go with Steve."

Terry shook her head. "I don't think anybody should go off alone," she said. "What if you got hurt?"

Mark started off, then stopped and looked

back. "Hey, Jordan. You're not going to let me down, are you?"

Jordan took his cue from Steve, who was grinning. With a shrug, Jordan followed Mark out of the clearing.

"I'll go too," Linda called out, running to catch up with them.

The rest of the group went with Steve, grumbling about how he'd probably picked the hardest route. "At least I picked a route," he said. "Mark didn't even do that. You'll see."

"Do you think they'll be able to find their way back?" Terry asked anxiously.

"If they can't, we'll hear them," Paul told her. "It seems like we're in the middle of nowhere, but really, the trails all wind around and run into each other, like Tim said."

Steve turned out to be right — there was a trail this way. Rachel wondered how long it would be before Mark and Jordan and Linda figured out they'd gone in the wrong direction. Or maybe there was another trail going their way and they'd all meet up in the middle.

They worked for a while, pulling away branches and undergrowth. It wasn't any worse than before, but they were getting tired and they moved more slowly. Every time Rachel stopped to rest for a minute, she looked up into the trees and saw that they were blowing harder than ever. Clouds were coming in, too. The blue sky she'd been able to see earlier was gray now.

"Did anyone hear anything about a storm?" she asked.

"How would we hear?" Stacey said. "I haven't been able to get a radio station yet. I brought my radio for nothing."

"It's getting cloudy," Rachel said. "I don't really want to be out here if lightning starts."

"Yeah, you're right," Steve agreed. "We should probably head back."

"What about the others?" Terry asked.

"Just start shouting," Paul said. "I'm surprised we haven't heard them before now, anyway."

"Too proud to admit they were wrong," Steve laughed. Tilting his head back, he shouted Mark's name at the top of his lungs.

They listened. Nothing. Steve hollered again.

Then they heard it. Linda's voice, calling for help. It was strange to hear her sounding so upset — she was usually so in charge of everything.

"I knew it," Terry whispered. "I knew someone would get hurt."

"You didn't know anything," Stacey

snapped. "Come on, let's go find out what's wrong."

Going back was much easier now that they'd cleared the way. They were able to run — which is what they did, reaching the spot where they'd separated from the others just a few minutes ago.

They stopped only a moment to catch their breath, and then they went on, crashing through the branches and vines where Mark and Linda and Jordan had gone. The three of them had done a lot of clearing, but it was obvious there was no trail this way. Why hadn't they stopped and come back? Rachel wondered. Couldn't they take a little kidding?

They could still hear Linda's voice calling for help. It became louder, so they knew they were getting closer. They stopped for a second and listened again.

"Come on!" Linda was shouting. "I can't get up without help!"

Then they heard Mark. "Jordan should be back real soon, Linda!" His voice was scared, but angry, too. "Stop yelling at me! There's nothing I can do!"

The others hurried on, and the voices got louder.

"What do you mean?" Linda shrieked. "I

need help! Just let go and come get me!"

"I can't do it, okay?" Mark's voice cracked. "Just wait!"

Rachel couldn't imagine what was happening. Where were they?

And why had Jordan left them if they were in trouble?

Paul was up in front, and Rachel was following him. She was busy trying to keep the whipping branches from hitting her in the eyes, so she almost didn't stop in time.

Suddenly, without warning, they were out of the trees and teetering at the top of a wall of rock, its rough surface stretching almost straight down to a dried, rocky streambed at least thirty feet below. Paul caught hold of Rachel's sleeve before she stumbled over the edge and they clung together for a moment. The others came up behind them more slowly.

About halfway down, Linda was crouched on a rocky ledge that jutted out about three feet. She wasn't in danger of falling, but she was holding on to her ankle and obviously couldn't climb up or down because of the pain.

Mark was above her, not very far from the top. He was standing on another ledge. The wall wasn't a wall, really. It was broken and crumbled enough to make climbing almost easy. But Mark wasn't moving. He was leaning back against the rock behind him as if he wanted to press himself into it.

Rachel didn't need to ask what had happened. Linda had fallen and hurt her ankle, and was waiting for Mark to come help her.

But because of his fear of heights, Mark was paralyzed. He couldn't go down or up. He was frozen.

Rachel could hear him breathing, rapid pants that didn't give him enough air. She didn't have to see his eyes to know how they looked. She knew they weren't pale anymore. They must be black, and filled with terror.

Linda raised her head and looked up. "Hey, the rescue squad!" she shouted, sounding very relieved. "I guess we won't be spending the night out here after all!"

Rachel saw Mark turn his head. He didn't look up, though. Looking up meant leaning out a little, and he was too afraid to do it. "You've got . . ." Mark's panting got faster. "You've got to get me out of here!"

"*You?*" Linda was shouting at Mark, angry and indignant. "I'm the one with a twisted ankle!"

Rachel turned to Paul. "He's in worse shape than Linda," she said quietly. "He's got . . . I don't know the word. He's afraid of heights."

Paul nodded. Then he let go of her arm and started down after Mark.

"Where's Jordan, that's all I'd like to know," Stacey said. "Why'd he go looking for us? He didn't need us."

Steve was scrambling over the edge now. "I'll go get Linda and help her the rest of the way down. We'll meet you guys back at the clearing."

By now, Paul had reached Mark. Rachel could hear him talking quietly and firmly. Telling Mark to take his hand and turn around, that he wasn't going to fall. Mark's panicked breathing carried up to the top, louder than ever.

"Let's go back now," Rachel suggested. "We're not doing any good here. And maybe we'll run into Jordan." She didn't like Mark, but she didn't want to stick around and watch his humiliating climb to the top, either.

Stacey wanted to stay, but Terry decided to go back to the clearing with Rachel. When they got there, they sat down on the ground, leaned against a tree, and waited. Paul and Stacey joined them a little while later. Mark came behind them, walking slowly, not meeting anyone's eyes.

Before anyone could say anything, there was a rustling in the trees and Jordan came into the clearing. "I don't believe it!" he said, breathing heavily. "I've been running around like crazy. I thought everybody had disappeared!" He took another deep breath and was about to explain what had happened, when Steve and Linda arrived.

Linda was limping, leaning on Steve and Stacey. "You're lucky," Steve said as he helped her sit down. "There's no swelling or anything."

"What happened?" Stacey asked, looking at Jordan. "Why did you go running off?"

Jordan shrugged, looking uncomfortable.

"I'll tell you," Linda said. "I fell. Mark started down after me, and Jordan said he'd go get help."

"How come?" Stacey asked. "Why not just help them yourself, Jordan?"

"What difference does it make?" Paul said. "It's over."

Mark hadn't said anything, he'd just been staring at the ground. Now he lifted his head and looked at Linda. "I wanted to come down and help you," he said. "I was . . . I was scared to do it. But I wanted to try." He looked away, into the distance. "I couldn't keep going. I tried telling myself there was nothing to be afraid of. I knew it was true. But I . . . I froze anyway."

"Oh," Linda said softly. "I forgot. Mark, I forgot that you're scared of heights. That's why you couldn't help me."

"Yeah. I was going to try again," Mark said. His face twisted. "But I couldn't make it."

Linda got up and went over to him, barely limping now. Now that the frightening incident had passed, and she was safely back in the clearing, she seemed calm, in control again. "I'm sorry," she said. "I just wasn't thinking. I'm so sorry."

Mark turned away from her. Linda's sympathy was the last thing he wanted, Rachel thought. She could see it in his eyes. He was even more humiliated, but he was angry, too. He'd never forgive Linda for her sympathy.

Chapter 21

I couldn't believe it. It just happened, all by itself. They don't know it yet, but the psycho has struck again!

I'm getting close to the end now. They don't know that yet, either. They don't know anything. It won't be long, though. I'll explain it all, and I'll see their faces change, hear them scream and beg and cry. I've waited so long, and now the waiting's almost over.

It's time to finish it.

By the time they got back to camp, the wind was stronger, and dark clouds were scudding across the sky, blotting out the sun. There was no rain yet, but they knew it was coming.

"Great, a storm," Stacey muttered as they split up to go to their cabins. "Just another great day at Camp Silverlake. I never wanted to take this job anyway. It was my parents who were all for it. Ha. Wait'll I tell them there's some psycho stalking everybody."

"The psycho hasn't stalked anybody for a while," Linda said. "If there was one, maybe he's gone."

"I'm still spooked." Shivering, Stacey looked up at the darkening sky. "I wish we could get out of here."

Rachel didn't say anything. She knew no psycho was stalking the camp, but if she told them what she thought — that it was one of the people here — it would just make things worse. And since she didn't know who it was, saying something could be dangerous.

"How's your ankle feeling, Linda?" Terry asked as Linda went into the cabin.

"I guess I was lucky — it hardly hurts now." Linda moved to her bed and sat down. "At first I thought you'd have to carry me back on a stretcher." She lay back and stretched her legs out.

"Poor Mark," Terry said. "Did you notice he didn't talk all the way back? I felt so sorry for him." Again, Rachel felt that Terry was holding back a smile.

"I don't think we should say anything more about it," Rachel said. "Didn't you see his face? He was completely humiliated."

"How come you're sticking up for him?"

Stacey asked. "I thought you couldn't stand him. Besides, he was stupid to try to climb down if he's so scared of heights. He humiliated himself."

"Okay." Rachel decided to drop it. "I'm really grungy," she said, staring down at her jeans and shirt. "I think I'll take a shower."

Grabbing some clean clothes, Rachel headed for the shower cabin. The wind was strong enough to get through the treetops today. It blew her hair into her eyes and mouth as she hurried along the path.

The water was hot again, and she stood under it until it ran out. Outside, she could hear the wind whistling, and the first low rumble of thunder in the distance.

When she was clean and dressed, she wrapped a towel around her wet hair and ran back to the cabin. The thunder rumbled again, closer now, but there was still no rain.

The cabin was empty when Rachel got back, and it was getting dark. She grabbed for the light string and pulled, automatically checking her bed to make sure no one had left another warning. Her bed was empty, too.

Relieved, Rachel toweled her hair dry and combed it. The others must have gone up to the lodge, she thought. It was five o'clock and almost time to eat, so maybe they were fixing dinner. After the work of clearing the trail, she was starving. She turned off the light and left the cabin.

Running along the path toward the lodge, Rachel saw Mr. Drummond out at the dock. He was checking on the boats, making sure they were tied securely. The boats were rocking and bobbing in the wind-whipped water.

Pulling open the big front door, Rachel dashed in. The wind almost tore the door from her hands, but Paul was in the entrance and helped her pull it shut. "Thanks," Rachel said. "It's getting wild out there."

"It's wild in here, too. Listen," Paul said.

Now Rachel could hear everyone's voices, coming from the kitchen. She heard Stacey shouting and Linda telling her to calm down. Mark kept saying, "It doesn't make sense," and Steve kept telling him killers didn't have to make sense.

"What is it?" Rachel asked.

Paul took her hand and tugged her over to the bulletin board. "Look at Mark's face," he said.

His voice told her what he'd seen, but Rachel looked anyway. Two circles again.

Mark had been a target.

Rachel felt a shiver of fear, but she was

confused, too. "Nothing happened to Mark. It was Linda who got hurt — she seemed pretty upset, too. I mean, Mark got scared and everything, but nothing really happened to him."

"I know," Paul agreed. "But somebody must have enjoyed the situation and drawn the circle. Like you, Linda doesn't have a picture up. Anyway, it's always the special things that scare people the most. Nobody's really been hurt, but they've been scared out of their wits."

"And humiliated," Rachel said.

The voices rose in the kitchen again.

"It's one of us," Rachel whispered, staring at the circled faces on the picture. "It really is one of us."

Everyone helped fix dinner, but it wasn't a friendly gathering. Now that everyone had seen the circles, they were more frightened than ever and their fear made them quiet. When they did talk, they snapped at each other.

Finally, Stacey slammed a handful of forks down on the counter. "I can't stand this!" she said, as one of the forks clattered to the floor. "Can't we just get out of here, at least for the night?"

"Tim and Michelle took the Jeep," Mark said. "The place is stocked with flashlights and lanterns, but no extra batteries, can you believe it? They wanted to get more in case we lose power tonight."

"Great." Stacey kicked at the fork and sent it skittering across the linoleum. "Now we're really stuck! How could they leave us here?"

"They don't know what's going on," Terry reminded her.

"This is just great!" Stacey shouted angrily. Then she stormed out of the kitchen.

Linda wiped her hands on a towel and followed her.

Jordan crossed his arms and leaned against a counter, looking down at his feet. Steve and Mark exchanged glances, then Mark went back to making a salad. Rachel watched his knife flash as it sliced through the head of lettuce.

It was the same knife that had been stuck in her bed.

It's one of us, she kept thinking.

Dinner was salad and hotdogs and it only took about twenty minutes to get ready. When they took the food and plates into the main room, they found Stacey curled up in a chair by the big fireplace.

"Up and at 'em, Stace," Steve said. "Food's ready."

Stacey uncurled herself and stood up. "Are those hotdogs boiled?"

"Just eat one and don't complain," Mark told her.

Rachel set pitchers of lemonade on the tables and started putting paper plates around. "Where's Linda?"

Stacey shrugged. "Out."

"Out?" Rachel put down the last plate. "Out where?"

"I don't know. She sat in here with me for a few minutes, and then she said she was going to take a walk."

"In this weather?" Terry asked. "There's a storm going on."

"Well, she said she liked it," Stacey said. "What's the big deal?"

Terry frowned at her. "The big deal is there may be lightning. And she's out there in it."

"Did she say where she was going?" Paul asked.

Stacey nodded, looking embarrassed now for letting Linda go. "On one of the trails," she told them. "The first one that branches off to the left of the main trail. We haven't been on that one yet, and she said she wanted to see what kind of shape it's in."

Before Stacey finished talking, the others were moving toward the door. "Where are you guys going?" she asked.

"Where do you think?" Mark said. "We're going to get her and bring her back. She was crazy to go out in the woods in this weather."

"Well, I don't want to stay here!" Stacey cried.

"Then get moving!" Steve called over his shoulder.

"Wait a sec," Paul stopped at the front door. "Somebody should stay here in case she comes back before we do. This could turn into a circus if she starts wandering around looking for us."

"I'll stay," Terry said quickly. "I'm afraid of storms anyway."

Terry turned back into the main room, and the rest of them headed out the door. It wasn't even six yet, but the sky was dark with rolling thunderclouds. Rachel could feel moisture in the air, but the rain hadn't started to really fall yet.

"Listen," Rachel said. The wind tore her voice away and she had to shout. "Listen, I'm going back to our cabin, just in case Linda's there!"

"Good idea!" Paul said. "We'll wait for you over by the main trail. If you two don't get there in say, five minutes, that means she's gone and we'll go ahead. If she's gone you might as well stay in the cabin, Rachel!" He grabbed her shoulder and kissed her quickly on the lips. "Hope I see you in five minutes, with Linda!"

Rachel smiled to herself as she watched him run off. Then the wind hit her hard in the back, as if to remind her why she was out here. She turned away and ran down the path toward her cabin.

The lake was a cold, silver-gray now, its surface rippling with waves that rose and fell onto the beach, washing the rocks until they glistened. The boats were bobbing wildly, banging against each other in the choppy water. Mr. Drummond wasn't there anymore, but Rachel saw a light in the storage cabin; maybe he'd decided to stay in there until the storm was over.

Off in the distance Rachel saw a fork of lightning snake down toward the ground. Then a loud thunderclap made her jump. She ran faster.

The cabin was still dark when she reached it, and she felt a stab of disappointment. If Linda was there, wouldn't she have turned the light on? But maybe not. Maybe she was just lying in the dark.

Calling Linda's name, Rachel ran into the cabin. No one answered. She pulled on the light and looked around, still hoping, but the cabin was empty.

Okay, Rachel thought. She'd wait there. She didn't like waiting, but it was stupid for everyone to go racing off into the woods.

How could Linda have gone into the woods in the middle of a thunderstorm? It was fine to enjoy wild weather, but it was crazy to go stand in the middle of it where she could get hit by branches. Or lightning.

Another loud thunderclap made Rachel jump again. Shivering, she pulled a sweatshirt on over her T-shirt and looked at the clock. It was six. Five minutes had gone by, she was sure of it. Paul and the others must be on the trail by now.

The wind was pouring in through the screens, making the window shades flap and rustle. There were shutters on the outside, but Rachel didn't feel like going out and closing them. She could read, she guessed, but she was too edgy to concentrate. She sat crosslegged on her bed and listened to the storm build.

A few more minutes went by, and then another gust of wind blew in so hard it scattered loose papers and candy wrappers across the floor. Rachel sighed. Okay, she'd close the shutters.

As she got off the bed, her foot landed on

one of the papers. She skidded a few inches, then bent down to pick it up. She almost crumpled it, but just before her hand closed into a fist, she looked down at it.

When she saw what it was, she tried to cry out, but the cry froze in her throat.

Chapter 22

How long will it take? Fifteen minutes? Twenty? I shouldn't be so impatient. After seven years, I can wait twenty more minutes.

It's going to be perfect. They have no idea. They think they're scared and worried now. But just wait. Just wait until I tell them. Wait until they hear. Then they'll know what fear really is.

I wonder exactly how it will end? That's the one thing I don't know. The one thing they'll have to tell me. They won't want to, but they will.

There they are. It's almost over. Now I'll find out the end.

It was a letter, written on white tablet paper. It had been folded hundreds of times and the folds were torn in places. It looked like the same letter, or one of them, that Rachel had seen Linda reading. But it wasn't from her boyfriend.

It was written in a rounded, childish hand. Not the handwriting of a young man. It was the handwriting of a boy.

A boy who signed his name *Johnny*.

> *Dear Linda,*
>
> *I wish I could come home. I don't get why they're so mean to me. I haven't done anything to them. Mark and Steve do the most stuff. Stacey does things, too. I think Jordan would stop if they did. But they won't. Tomorrow we go on the big hike. I have to be in the same tent with those guys and I know they are going to do something to me. It will be the worst. I'm not kidding. They told me.*
>
> *I really want to come home. I don't care if there're only five more days left. I know Mom and Dad are on a trip. You could talk to Mrs. Sanderson. She could call and pretend to be Mom. Or you could. Tell them to send me home. Okay?*
>
> *Love,*
> *Johnny*

There were other letters, too. Rachel found them in Linda's duffel bag, three more letters that told how unhappy Johnny was. How Mark and Steve, Stacey and Jordan had teased him and played dirty tricks on him. Just like Paul said. The letters didn't mention Paul. They didn't mention any counselors. Hadn't Johnny talked to the counselors? Maybe the others had warned him not to, and he was too afraid.

Linda's bag had Johnny's picture in it, too. The one Rachel had put on the bulletin board.

She was his sister, Rachel thought. Linda and Johnny were brother and sister. Was Linda's last name really Duncan, or had she made it up? Maybe they had different fathers, or Linda used her mother's name, it didn't matter. Johnny had written to his sister, asking to come home, asking her to help because their parents were away. Who was Mrs. Sanderson? A sitter, a housekeeper; that didn't matter either. Linda must have been about eleven then, only a year or so older than Johnny. She tried, Rachel knew she must have tried, but she was too young.

Nobody listened.

And Johnny died.

But Linda was going to make them listen now.

She was going to make them pay.

With shaking hands, Rachel stuffed one of the letters in her pocket. Then she grabbed a flashlight and raced out of the cabin.

The rain had started now, but it wasn't very heavy yet. The wind plastered Rachel's hair across her eyes and mouth; she had to keep peeling it away so she could see and breathe.

She looked for the Jeep, but it wasn't there. Michelle and Tim weren't back yet.

Stop and get Terry? No, let her stay there. It was safe there.

She thought she heard someone shouting at her. A deep voice. Mr. Drummond. She wanted to stop and explain, but there wasn't time.

If she hurried, if she ran faster than she'd ever run, she might catch up to them.

What would Linda do? What did she have planned? Whatever it was, it would be Jordan this time. Jordan was the only one left.

It must have been so hard. Images of Linda flashed through Rachel's mind as she left the campground and started along the main trail. Linda smiling and laughing. Linda the organizer. Seeing the picture on the bulletin board. Suggesting that they pretend to be Johnny's ghost. When Rachel talked about Johnny, it must have been so hard for Linda to keep pretending.

When Rachel got to the trail Stacey had

talked about, she had to stop and catch her breath. The thunder was still booming, and she heard a loud crack. Lightning. But she couldn't see it. The trees were too thick. As long as she couldn't see it, she wouldn't let it scare her.

It was dim in the trees and she turned on the flashlight. She took a few more deep breaths and then she started running again, not knowing what she'd find at the end of the trail. Only Linda knew that.

They'd never taken this trail, but Rachel could see where the others had gone before her. Branches and vines had been pushed to the side, making her way easier. Her flashlight beam dipped and bobbed in the spruce and pine trees. Raindrops dripped from the branches and rolled down her neck and face. She could hear the wind, whistling furiously in the tree-tops, but it couldn't touch her.

Had Johnny died on a night like this? Listening to the wind, feeling the rain, running scared through the trees until he stumbled and fell to his death?

Rachel stopped again. She'd heard something. As if it could make her hear better, she snapped off the flashlight and listened.

Voices. Stacey and Steve. And Mark. Panicked.

And Linda. Linda's voice riding over the rest

of them. "Tell me! Tell me exactly what happened! I'm his sister, I have a right to know!"

Hoping the wind and thunder would mask any noise she made, Rachel crept forward. She stepped over fallen branches, tripped on some vines, but finally she got close enough to see.

She could see down into a deep gully. There was a dead, uprooted tree at the bottom. It was decaying now, but Rachel remembered what Paul had said.

She knew it must be the same one Johnny had fallen against when he died.

Steve and Mark and Stacey were down in the gully, standing next to the tree trunk.

Up top, looking down on them, were Paul and Jordan.

And Linda. Even in the dim light, her bright, coppery hair shone like a beacon.

In her hands was a gun, the long-barreled rifle from the storage cabin.

She swung it back and forth, down to the gully, then back up to Paul and Jordan.

"Tell me!" she said again.

"Okay!" Steve gasped. "Okay, we'll tell you! Mark and I, we made him go out that night. We drew straws. Well, sticks. And we made sure he lost. We told him somebody always had to leave the tent and check to make sure Mr. Drummond wasn't coming. We got him scared of Mr. Drummond, see." He stopped, swallowing hard.

"It was easy, because Drummond was so creepy," Stacey said, picking up the story. "Everybody was scared of him." Her lips quivered and she couldn't go on.

"There were noises," Mark said. "There're always noises in the woods, and it was raining anyway. We told him it might be Drummond. We told him he had to go out and see."

"Or what?" Linda shouted. "Why did he go? How did you make him go?"

"We promised him we wouldn't do anything to him anymore!" Mark went on in a rush. "He just had to do this one thing and then we'd never bother him again!"

They *made* him go out that night, Rachel thought.

No wonder they felt guilty. One of their tricks had led to his death.

Maybe *they'd* put the dead snake on her bed. Maybe that's why it had seemed different. They couldn't use her phobias against her because she didn't have any, not really. But it *was* a warning. They were afraid she'd find out. They wanted to frighten her so she'd shut up about Johnny.

Rachel wondered if they would have kept

their promise to him, about it being the last trick. She felt sick.

But Linda was laughing, a harsh, ragged laugh with no humor in it. "And he believed you!" she said to Mark. "That's why he left the tent. He was so desperate to have you stop, he would have jumped off a cliff if you'd promised to stop!"

Jump off a cliff.

The words seemed to echo.

Linda stopped laughing and swung the rifle toward Jordan. "That's almost what Johnny did, isn't it Jordan? Except he didn't jump, did he?"

Jordan stood rigid. "We didn't think . . ." he said through stiff lips. "We never meant for him to get hurt."

"He didn't just get hurt, Jordan." Linda's voice was raspy. "He broke his neck. He died."

Only Jordan's eyes moved, darting back and forth, looking for a way out.

"Okay,' Linda said. "It's your turn, Jordan. Johnny wrote me about you. He said he thought you wouldn't bother him if the others didn't. You just went along, didn't you?"

Whichever way the wind blew, Rachel thought.

"They took the lead and you followed," Linda

went on. "It was easier that way. You didn't have to think about what was right. It would have been too hard. You just followed the crowd."

A bolt of lightning lit up the forest, bathing everyone's faces in white light for a second.

Rachel saw their eyes, wide and frightened. When the thunder came, she scrambled closer. She didn't know what she was going to do, but she needed to be closer. It was cold now, but she could feel the sweat beading her face. Her heart was drumming in her ears, as loud as the thunder. She crouched down and listened.

"It's your turn, Jordan," Linda said again. "You take the lead this time. No waiting to see what everyone else is going to do. You decide."

"Decide what?"

Linda swung the rifle toward the three down in the gully. "Them?" she said. Then she swung it toward Paul. "Or him?"

Jordan's lips moved, but he couldn't get the words out for a moment. Finally he managed to stammer, "I don't . . . I don't get it."

"Oh, you get it, Jordan." Linda swung the rifle back and forth again. "Come on. It's your decision."

Jordan shook his head. Everyone else was silent.

"Okay, I'll make it a little easier. Which one

of them should I kill?" Linda pointed the rifle at Jordan. "Or should I just kill you?"

Jordan flinched and took a step backward. "This is crazy," he said. "We didn't kill your brother. We didn't drag him out and throw him down there. It's not the same thing."

"It is to me!" Linda shouted. "He was worth all of you to me! Come on, Jordan, decide! Decide!"

Linda was advancing on Jordan, the rifle pointed right at him. Her amber eyes were wide and gleaming; a strand of red hair swept across her throat like a flame. She kept moving toward him.

Rachel knew Linda was about to make the decision herself.

If Rachel wanted to save them, she had to act fast.

Rising quickly, Rachel drew back her arm and hurled the flashlight through the air.

It didn't hit Linda, but it stopped her. Startled, she swung in Rachel's direction. Rachel saw the barrel of the rifle pointing at her. Screaming once, she threw herself to the ground, waiting for the sound of a gunshot.

Instead, she heard Paul's voice. "It's over. It's over, Linda! You can't do anything more!"

Then Rachel heard Linda crying.

Slowly, Rachel got to her feet.

Paul was holding the rifle, its barrel pointing toward the ground. Mark and Stacey and Steve were climbing out of the gully. Jordan took their hands and helped them up the last few feet.

Linda was standing alone, her head down. "I wouldn't have shot them," she said in a broken voice. "I just wanted to scare them. I wanted them to know how it felt."

Rachel heard someone behind her. Turning, she saw Mr. Drummond. She didn't know how long he'd been there. She hadn't heard him until now. The groundskeeper moved past her, branches crackling under his weight. Striding quickly to Paul, he took the rifle from him. "It's not loaded," he said. "I never keep it loaded. Too dangerous." He looked at Linda and his face seemed to soften. "Johnny was a nice boy," he said.

Linda nodded, crying quietly now.

Mr. Drummond took her arm. He tugged gently, and she walked with him, past Rachel and back onto the trail.

Rachel's legs felt shaky. She sat down quickly, drawing her knees up and wrapping her arms around them.

Stacey was crying, and Steve put his arm around her. She shook him off, but then threw herself against him and sobbed. Mark patted

Steve's shoulder. Jordan moved closer to them, waiting to be noticed, waiting to see if they'd include him. Mark held out his hand and Jordan grasped it. Clinging together, they all moved awkwardly toward the trail. Steve touched Paul's shoulder as they passed him. Mark's pale eyes looked down on Rachel and he smiled crookedly.

When the four of them were gone, Paul walked over to Rachel and held out his hand. Rachel took it and got to her feet.

"You're okay?" he said, holding her close.

Rachel nodded, her face against his shoulder. She stayed that way for a minute, then she pulled away and looked at him. "What about Linda? Do you think she'll be all right?"

"I don't know," he said. "Maybe. After a while." He shivered a little. "Why did you come here? Not that I'm complaining," he said with a smile. "I just wondered."

Rachel dug into her pocket and pulled out the letter from Johnny. "I found this in the cabin," she explained. "He wrote her and told her what was happening. And who was doing it."

Paul took the letter and read it. "Seven years," he said, handing the letter back. "She's been holding this grudge for seven years."

"She said she wanted to scare them, so

they'd know how it felt." Rachel put the letter back in her pocket. "She did it, didn't she? They won't ever forget."

"No." Paul put his arm around her. "She did what she planned. But it's finished now. So maybe at least *she* can forget."

Rachel put her arm around his waist, and they started back to camp. It was still raining, but not very hard, and the thunder was just a low rumble in the distance now. The worst of the storm was over. The wind had died down, and they couldn't feel it. But they could hear it blowing gently high up in the tops of the pines.

About the Author

Carol Ellis is the author of more than twenty books for young people, including *The Stepdaughter*, *The Window*, *My Secret Admirer*, and the short story, "The Doll" in *Thirteen*. While she doesn't read horror books herself, some of her favorite reading is mystery and suspense, especially those books in which an ordinary, innocent person becomes caught up in something strange and frightening.

Carol Ellis lives in New York State with her husband and their son.

THRILLERS

R.L. Stine
- ❏ MC44236-8 The Baby-sitter $3.50
- ❏ MC44332-1 The Baby-sitter II $3.50
- ❏ MC45386-6 Beach House $3.25
- ❏ MC43278-8 Beach Party $3.50
- ❏ MC43125-0 Blind Date $3.50
- ❏ MC43279-6 The Boyfriend $3.50
- ❏ MC44333-X The Girlfriend $3.50
- ❏ MC45385-8 Hit and Run $3.25
- ❏ MC46100-1 The Hitchhiker $3.50
- ❏ MC43280-X The Snowman $3.50
- ❏ MC43139-0 Twisted $3.50

Caroline B. Cooney
- ❏ MC44316-X The Cheerleader $3.25
- ❏ MC41641-3 The Fire $3.25
- ❏ MC43806-9 The Fog $3.25
- ❏ MC45681-4 Freeze Tag $3.25
- ❏ MC45402-1 The Perfume $3.25
- ❏ MC44884-6 The Return of the Vampire $2.95
- ❏ MC41640-5 The Snow $3.25
- ❏ MC45682-2 The Vampire's Promise $3.50

Diane Hoh
- ❏ MC44330-5 The Accident $3.25
- ❏ MC45401-3 The Fever $3.25
- ❏ MC43050-5 Funhouse $3.25
- ❏ MC44904-4 The Invitation $3.50
- ❏ MC45640-7 The Train (9/92) $3.25

Sinclair Smith
- ❏ MC45063-8 The Waitress $2.95

Christopher Pike
- ❏ MC43014-9 Slumber Party $3.50
- ❏ MC44256-2 Weekend $3.50

A. Bates
- ❏ MC45829-9 The Dead Game $3.25
- ❏ MC43291-5 Final Exam $3.25
- ❏ MC44582-0 Mother's Helper $3.50
- ❏ MC44238-4 Party Line $3.25

D.E. Athkins
- ❏ MC45246-0 Mirror, Mirror $3.25
- ❏ MC45349-1 The Ripper $3.25
- ❏ MC44941-9 Sister Dearest $2.95

Carol Ellis
- ❏ MC44768-8 My Secret Admirer $3.25
- ❏ MC46044-7 The Stepdaughter $3.25
- ❏ MC44916-8 The Window $2.95

Richie Tankersley Cusick
- ❏ MC43115-3 April Fools $3.25
- ❏ MC43203-6 The Lifeguard $3.25
- ❏ MC43114-5 Teacher's Pet $3.25
- ❏ MC44235-X Trick or Treat $3.25

Lael Littke
- ❏ MC44237-6 Prom Dress $3.25

Edited by T. Pines
- ❏ MC45256-8 Thirteen $3.50

Available wherever you buy books, or use this order form.

Scholastic Inc., P.O. Box 7502, 2931 East McCarty Street, Jefferson City, MO 65102

Please send me the books I have checked above. I am enclosing $_____ (please add $2.00 to cover shipping and handling). Send check or money order — no cash or C.O.D.s please.

Name _____

Address_____

City_____ State/Zip_____
Please allow four to six weeks for delivery. Offer good in the U.S. only. Sorry, mail orders are not available to residents of Canada. Prices subject to change.   PT1092

THRILLERS

Nobody Scares 'Em Like R.L. Stine